**Aesop,** according to legend, was born either in Sardis, on the Greek island of Samos, or in Cotiaeum, the chief city in a province of Phrygia, and lived from about 620 to 560 B.C. Little is known about his life, but Aristotle mentioned his acting as a public defender, and Plutarch numbered him as one of the "Seven Wise Men." It is generally believed he was a slave, freed by his master because of his wit and wisdom. As a free man, he went to Athens, ruled at that time by the tyrant Peisistratus, an enemy of free speech. As Aesop became famous for his fables, which used animals as a code to tell the truth about political injustice, he incurred the wrath of Peisistratus. Eventually, Aesop was condemned to death for sacrilege and thrown over a cliff. Later, the Athenians erected a statue in his honor. In about 300 B.C., Demetrius Phalereus of Athens made the first known collection of Aesop's fables, which then spread far beyond the Greek world.

**Jack Zipes** is a professor of German at the University of Minnesota. He is the author of several books of fairy tales, including *Breaking the Magic Spell* and *Don't Bet on the Prince.* He is also the editor of several volumes of fairy tales, including *Beauties, Beasts and Enchantment: Classic French Fairy Tales, The Fairy Tales of Oscar Wilde, The Fairy Tales of Frank Stockton,* and *Arabian Nights.*

**Sam Pickering** teaches English at the University of Connecticut. He has written seventeen books, fourteen of which are collections of essays. His most recent books are *Waltzing the Magpies,* an account of a year he and his family spent in Western Australia, and *The Best of Pickering,* both published by the University of Michigan Press.

# FABLES

# AESOP'S FABLES

EDITED AND WITH AN AFTERWORD BY

JACK ZIPES

WITH A NEW INTRODUCTION BY

SAM PICKERING

SIGNET CLASSICS
Published by New American Library, a division of
Penguin Group (USA) Inc., 375 Hudson Street,
New York, New York 10014, USA
Penguin Group (Canada), 90 Eglinton Avenue East, Suite 700, Toronto,
Ontario M4P 2Y3, Canada (a division of Pearson Penguin Canada Inc.)
Penguin Books Ltd., 80 Strand, London WC2R 0RL, England
Penguin Ireland, 25 St. Stephen's Green, Dublin 2,
Ireland (a division of Penguin Books Ltd.)
Penguin Group (Australia), 250 Camberwell Road, Camberwell, Victoria 3124,
Australia (a division of Pearson Australia Group Pty. Ltd.)
Penguin Books India Pvt. Ltd., 11 Community Centre, Panchsheel Park,
New Delhi - 110 017, India
Penguin Group (NZ), 67 Apollo Drive, Rosedale, North Shore 0632,
New Zealand (a division of Pearson New Zealand Ltd.)
Penguin Books (South Africa) (Pty.) Ltd., 24 Sturdee Avenue,
Rosebank, Johannesburg 2196, South Africa

Penguin Books Ltd., Registered Offices:
80 Strand, London WC2R 0RL, England

Published by Signet Classics, an imprint of New American Library,
a division of Penguin Group (USA) Inc.

First Signet Classics Printing, October 1992
First Signet Classics Printing (Pickering Introduction), October 2004
10 9 8

Printed in the United States of America

# Contents


| | | |
|---|---|---|
| | A Note on the Text and Illustrations | xiii |
| | Introduction | 3 |
| I | The Fox and the Grapes | 15 |
| II | The Wolf and the Crane | 17 |
| III | The Archer and the Lion | 18 |
| IV | The Woman and the Fat Hen | 19 |
| V | The Kid and the Wolf | 20 |
| VI | The Hawk and the Pigeons | 21 |
| VII | The Eagle and the Fox | 22 |
| VIII | The Boy and the Scorpion | 23 |
| IX | The Fox and the Goat | 25 |
| X | The Old Hound | 26 |
| XI | The Ants and the Grasshopper | 27 |
| XII | The Fawn and Her Mother | 28 |
| XIII | The Horse and the Groom | 29 |
| XIV | The Mountain in Labor | 31 |
| XV | The Flies and the Honey Jar | 32 |
| XVI | The Two Bags | 33 |
| XVII | The Vain Crow | 35 |
| XVIII | The Wolf and the Lamb | 37 |
| XIX | The Bear and the Fox | 38 |
| XX | The Dog, the Cock, and the Fox | 39 |

| | | |
|---|---|---|
| XXI | The Cock and the Jewel | 41 |
| XXII | The Sea Gull and the Hawk | 42 |
| XXIII | The Fox and the Lion | 43 |
| XXIV | The Creaking Wheels | 44 |
| XXV | The Frog and the Ox | 45 |
| XXVI | The Farmer and the Snake | 46 |
| XXVII | The Lion and the Fox | 47 |
| XXVIII | The Fisherman and His Music | 49 |
| XXIX | The Domesticated Dog and the Wolf | 50 |
| XXX | The Country Mouse and the Town Mouse | 53 |
| XXXI | The Dog and the Shadow | 55 |
| XXXII | The Moon and Her Mother | 56 |
| XXXIII | The Fighting Cocks and the Eagle | 57 |
| XXXIV | The Man and the Satyr | 59 |
| XXXV | The Tortoise and the Eagle | 60 |
| XXXVI | The Mule | 61 |
| XXXVII | The Hen and the Cat | 62 |
| XXXVIII | The Old Woman and the Wine Bottle | 63 |
| XXXIX | The Hare and the Tortoise | 65 |
| XL | The Ass and the Grasshopper | 66 |
| XLI | The Lamb and the Wolf | 67 |
| XLII | The Crab and Its Mother | 68 |
| XLIII | Jupiter and the Camel | 69 |
| XLIV | The Mouse and the Frog | 71 |
| XLV | The Shepherd Boy and the Wolf | 72 |
| XLVI | The Peach, the Apple, and the Blackberry | 73 |

| | | |
|---|---|---|
| XLVII | The Hare and the Hound | 74 |
| XLVIII | The Stag in the Ox Stall | 75 |
| XLIX | The Crow and the Pitcher | 77 |
| L | The Lion and the Mouse | 79 |
| LI | The One-Eyed Doe | 80 |
| LII | The Trees and the Ax | 81 |
| LIII | The Lion, the Ass, and the Fox Who Went Hunting | 83 |
| LIV | The Travelers and the Bear | 84 |
| LV | The Belly and the Members | 85 |
| LVI | The Dolphins and the Sprat | 86 |
| LVII | The Blind Man and the Whelp | 87 |
| LVIII | The Sick Stag | 89 |
| LIX | Hercules and the Wagoner | 90 |
| LX | The Fox and the Woodcutter | 91 |
| LXI | The Monkey and the Camel | 92 |
| LXII | The Dove and the Crow | 93 |
| LXIII | The Ass and the Lap Dog | 95 |
| LXIV | The Hares and the Frogs | 96 |
| LXV | The Fisherman and the Little Fish | 97 |
| LXVI | The Wind and the Sun | 98 |
| LXVII | The Farmer and the Stork | 99 |
| LXVIII | The Lioness | 101 |
| LXIX | The Brash Candlelight | 102 |
| LXX | The Old Woman and the Physician | 103 |
| LXXI | The Charcoal-Burner and the Cloth-Fuller | 104 |
| LXXII | The Wolf and the Sheep | 105 |
| LXXIII | The Farmer and His Sons | 107 |

| | | |
|---|---|---|
| LXXIV | The Wolves and the Sheep | 109 |
| LXXV | The Mole and Her Mother | 110 |
| LXXVI | The Swallow and the Crow | 111 |
| LXXVII | The Man Bitten by a Dog | 112 |
| LXXVIII | The Man and the Lion | 113 |
| LXXIX | The Monkey and the Dolphin | 115 |
| LXXX | The Dog and His Master | 116 |
| LXXXI | The Viper and the File | 117 |
| LXXXII | The Bundle of Sticks | 118 |
| LXXXIII | Jupiter, Neptune, Minerva, and Momus | 119 |
| LXXXIV | The Lion in Love | 121 |
| LXXXV | The Nurse and the Wolf | 122 |
| LXXXVI | The Birdcatcher and the Lark | 123 |
| LXXXVII | Jupiter and the Bee | 124 |
| LXXXVIII | The Travelers and the Plane Tree | 125 |
| LXXXIX | The Fox Without a Tail | 127 |
| XC | The Horse and the Stag | 128 |
| XCI | The Mischievous Dog | 129 |
| XCII | The Geese and the Cranes | 130 |
| XCIII | The Quack Frog | 131 |
| XCIV | Mercury and the Woodcutter | 133 |
| XCV | The Oxen and the Butchers | 135 |
| XCVI | The Goatherd and the Goats | 136 |
| XCVII | The Widow and the Sheep | 137 |
| XCVIII | The Marriage of the Sun | 138 |
| XCIX | The Thief and His Mother | 139 |
| C | The Gnat and the Bull | 140 |
| CI | The Lion, the Bear, and the Fox | 141 |

| | | |
|---|---|---|
| CII | The Oak and the Reed | 143 |
| CIII | The Dog in the Manger | 144 |
| CIV | The Goose with the Golden Eggs | 145 |
| CV | The Lion and the Dolphin | 146 |
| CVI | The Comedian and the Farmer | 147 |
| CVII | The Dog Invited to Supper | 149 |
| CVIII | The Ass Loaded with Salt | 151 |
| CIX | The Thief and the Dog | 152 |
| CX | The Trumpeter Taken Prisoner | 153 |
| CXI | The Hunter and the Fisherman | 154 |
| CXII | The Fir Tree and the Bramble | 155 |
| CXIII | The Eagle and the Arrow | 157 |
| CXIV | The Two Pots | 158 |
| CXV | The Fisherman and Troubled Water | 159 |
| CXVI | The Lark and Her Young Ones | 161 |
| CXVII | The Arab and the Camel | 163 |
| CXVIII | The Travelers and the Hatchet | 164 |
| CXIX | The Doctor and His Patient | 165 |
| CXX | The Maid and the Pail of Milk | 167 |
| CXXI | The Ass, the Fox, and the Lion | 168 |
| CXXII | The Ass and His Driver | 169 |
| CXXIII | The Birds, the Beasts, and the Bat | 170 |
| CXXIV | The Hedge and the Vineyard | 171 |
| CXXV | The Frogs Who Desired a King | 173 |
| CXXVI | The Lion and the Goat | 175 |
| CXXVII | The Mice in Council | 177 |
| CXXVIII | The Fox and the Mask | 178 |
| CXXIX | The Thirsty Pigeon | 179 |

| | | |
|---|---|---|
| CXXX | The Farmer and the Cranes | 180 |
| CXXXI | The Falconer and the Partridge | 181 |
| CXXXII | The Cat and the Mice | 183 |
| CXXXIII | The Father and His Two Daughters | 184 |
| CXXXIV | The Heifer and the Ox | 185 |
| CXXXV | The Fox and the Hedgehog | 187 |
| CXXXVI | The Lion and the Ass | 188 |
| CXXXVII | The Bald Knight | 189 |
| CXXXVIII | The Ass and His Masters | 191 |
| CXXXIX | The Farmer and the Sea | 192 |
| CXL | The Hart and the Vine | 193 |
| CXLI | The Pig and the Sheep | 194 |
| CXLII | The Bull and the Goat | 195 |
| CXLIII | The Old Man and Death | 197 |
| CXLIV | The Dog and the Hare | 198 |
| CXLV | The Boy and the Hazel Nuts | 199 |
| CXLVI | The Wolf and the Shepherd | 201 |
| CXLVII | The Jackass and the Statue | 202 |
| CXLVIII | The Blacksmith and His Dog | 203 |
| CXLIX | The Herdsman and the Lost Calf | 204 |
| CL | The Lion and the Other Beasts Who Went Out Hunting | 205 |
| CLI | The Bees, the Drones, and the Wasp | 207 |
| CLII | The Kid and the Piping Wolf | 208 |
| CLIII | The Stallion and the Ass | 209 |
| CLIV | The Mice and the Weasels | 211 |
| CLV | The Stubborn Goat and the Goatherd | 212 |

CLVI The Boys and the Frogs 213
CLVII The Mouse and the Weasel 214
CLVIII The Farmer and the Lion 215
CLIX The Horse and the Loaded Ass 217
CLX The Wolf and the Lion 218
CLXI The Farmer and the Dogs 219
CLXII The Eagle and the Crow 221
CLXIII The Lion and His Three Councillors 222
CLXIV The Great and Little Fish 223
CLXV The Ass, the Cock, and the Lion 224
CLXVI The Wolf and the Goat 225
CLXVII The Fox and the Stork 227
CLXVIII The Leopard and the Fox 228
CLXIX The Vine and the Goat 229
CLXX The Sick Lion 231
CLXXI The Rivers and the Sea 232
CLXXII The Blackamoor 233
CLXXIII The Boy and the Nettle 234
CLXXIV The Seaside Travelers 235
CLXXV The Boy Who Went Swimming 237
CLXXVI The Sick Hawk 238
CLXXVII The Monkey and the Fishermen 239
CLXXVIII Venus and the Cat 241
CLXXIX The Three Tradesmen 242
CLXXX The Ass's Shadow 243
CLXXXI The Eagle and the Beetle 245
CLXXXII The Lion and the Three Bulls 247
CLXXXIII The Old Woman and Her Maids 248

| | | |
|---|---|---|
| CLXXXIV | The Dogs and the Hides | 249 |
| CLXXXV | The Dove and the Ant | 251 |
| CLXXXVI | The Old Lion | 252 |
| CLXXXVII | The Wolf and the Shepherds | 253 |
| CLXXXVIII | The Ass in the Lion's Skin | 255 |
| CLXXXIX | The Swallow in Chancery | 256 |
| CXC | The Raven and the Swan | 257 |
| CXCI | The Wild Boar and the Fox | 258 |
| CXCII | The Stag at the Pool | 259 |
| CXCIII | The Wolf in Sheep's Clothing | 260 |
| CXCIV | The Boasting Traveler | 261 |
| CXCV | The Man and His Two Wives | 263 |
| CXCVI | The Shepherd and the Sea | 265 |
| CXCVII | The Miser | 267 |
| CXCVIII | Mercury and the Sculptor | 268 |
| CXCIX | The Miller, His Son, and Their Ass | 269 |
| CC | The Wolf and the Horse | 271 |
| CCI | The Astronomer | 272 |
| CCII | The Hunter and the Woodcutter | 273 |
| CCIII | The Fox and the Crow | 275 |
| | Afterword | 276 |
| | Selected Bibliography | 284 |
| | Index | 286 |

# A Note on the Text and Illustrations

This edition of *Aesop's Fables* is based on the Reverend Thomas James's *Aesop's Fables: A New Version, Chiefly from Original Sources* (New York: Robert B. Collins, 1848). While adapting this version of the fables, I consulted numerous other nineteenth-century translations and made various changes in keeping with the traditional plots. As has been the custom with translators and adapters of Aesop's fables, I have taken a good deal of poetic license at times. Since Mr. James's style is somewhat archaic, I have used a more modern American idiom in adapting them and have occasionally conceived new morals so that the fables might ring more "true" to the situation of the contemporary reader.

The illustrations are from *Fables de La Fontaine* illustrated by J.J. Grandville (Paris: H. Fournier, 1838). Grandville was a pseudonym for Jean Ignace Isidore Gérard (1803–1847). Born in Nancy, he arrived in Paris during the 1820s and soon made a name for himself as a lithographer and political caricaturist. He was especially interested the theater and animals and was known for incorporating political satire into his complex and fastidious drawings. During the 1830s he turned to book illustration and composed 120 woodcuts for La Fontaine's fables, which were largely based on Aesop's work; he caused quite a stir by turning many of the animals into types of human beings. In doing this, Grandville's figures often appear grotesque and have a surreal quality to them. The distinction between beast and human is blurred, or rather, Grandville's keen eye captures stunning similarities between humans and animals that often make humans appear in a ridiculous light. In addition, Grandville takes pains to give a clear indication of the social status of the figures through their clothing and behavior to comment on the French mores of his time. There are many emblematic references to urban life in Paris, and in this respect Grandville was one of the first artists to address modern problems of the city and industrialization. Grandville also illustrated the *Fables de S. Lavalette* (1841) and the *Fables de Florian* (1842), two minor French fabulists, in the same unique manner and is considered one of the greatest interpreters of Aesop's fables (through La Fontaine) for the modern age.

—J.Z.

# AESOP'S FABLES

# Introduction

Little is known about Aesop, except that he lived in Greece, probably between 600 and 500 B.C. Happily for readers, scribblers can rarely resist adorning empty biographies with tales—appropriate in Aesop's case, since generations have celebrated him as the archetypal storyteller. "What Aesop was by birth," Nathaniel Crouch wrote in 1737, "authors don't agree, but that he was of a mean condition, and his person deformed to the highest degree, is what all affirm: he was flat-nos'd, hunch-back'd, bloober-lip'd, jolt-headed: his body crooked all over, big-belly'd, badger-legg'd, and of a swarthy complexion. But the excellency and beauty of his mind made a sufficient atonement for the outward appearance of his person." Add that he stuttered terribly, quite a handicap for a philosophic raconteur, and Aesop becomes a man delightful to discover on the page, no matter the quality of his mind.

Fictional accounts of Aesop's life usually relate that he was sold as a slave in Ephesus. Later, in Samos, he behaved like Solomon, his wisdom reconciling the irreconcilable. After accusing magistrates at Delos of tomfoolery and corruption, however, he met a stony end. A gold cup pilfered from the shrine to the Oracle having been planted in his baggage, he was convicted of sacrilege and tossed "head-long from a high rock." The moral being, I suppose, the wages of tale-telling will out.

In the literary underworld, lie and truth twine fruitfully together through generations, spawning page after page. Crouch lifted his life from the introduction of Roger L'Estrange's famous collection of some five hundred fables published in 1692. In his collection published in 1722, Samuel Croxall took L'Estrange to task, declaring, "There were never so many blunders and childish dreams mixt up together, as are to be met with in the short compass of that piece." Knowing "the little trifling circumstances" of Aesop's life, Croxall said, was insignificant, "whether he was a slave or a freeman, whether handsome or ugly. He has left us a legacy in his writings that will preserve his memory clean and perpetual among us."

Croxall also got matters wrong. Aesop told but did not write down fables. Much as *The Thousand and One Nights* is a miscellany of stories drawn from diverse cultures stretching from Egypt to China, so the origins of Aesop's fables are various, all editions being mongrel blends of tales taken from countries around the Mediterranean and to the east.

What is true is that in 1484, when William Caxton printed his collection, the fables entered English. Caxton's edition was not meant for children. By the eighteenth century, however, the fables had practically become material for a children's book, first as a textbook for teaching languages (English and French, then primarily Latin and Greek) and second simply as children's literature combining entertainment with moral instruction. Before the reign of Queen Anne, the *Guardian of Education* declared in 1802, "very few" books were written expressly for children. The "first period" of "Juvenile Literature," the journal explained, began after John Locke popularized the idea of linking amusement with instruction. In his *Some Thoughts Concerning Education* (1693) and his closely related *Essay Concerning Human Understanding* (1690), Locke provided the seventeenth century with a scientific basis for the study of human development and an explanation of the formative importance of education. Nine people out of ten, he argued, were formed good or evil, useful or not, by education. For Locke, and educators who followed him, the child became the father or mother of the adult. The little and "almost insensible impressions on our tender infancies," Locke wrote, had "very important and lasting consequences." Moreover, Locke noted, a child's mind resembled a "white paper void of all characters." By implication, if parents or teachers managed the impressions that marked the white paper, they could control development and ultimately determine both a child's moral and financial success.

What children read suddenly became educationally significant. Learning, Locke wrote, should "be made a play and recreation to children." To this end he urged the invention of "play-things" in order to cozen children into studying the alphabet. Once children began to read, "some easy pleasant book" suited to their capacities should be given to them as "bait." Locke criticized old wives' and fairy tales, saying it was crucial that books not fill children's heads "with perfect useless trumpery, or lay the principles of vice and folly." For young readers he recommended Aesop's fables. Not only were the "stories apt to delight and entertain a child," but they also afforded "useful reflections to a grown man." In later years, he said, adults would not repent finding the stories impressed upon their memories among their "manly thoughts and serious business."

Locke also suggested that a child read an edition of Aesop with "pictures in it." The book, he wrote, "will entertain him much the better, and encourage him to read, when it carries the increase of knowledge with it." By the nineteenth century, illustrations probably contributed as much to the success of particular editions as the fables themselves. John Tenniel, Randolph Caldecott, Walter Crane, and Arthur Rackham were among a host of artists who illustrated editions for children. Of the seventeenth- and eighteenth-century collections, the best and most interesting illustrated editions are Francis Barlow's *Aesop's Fables with His Life: In English, French & Latin* (1666), that of Croxall published in 1722, Robert Dodsley's *Select Fables of Esop and Other Fabulists* (1761), and Thomas Saint's *Select Fables, in Three Parts*, illustrated by Thomas Bewick (1784).

Despite statements typically declaring that the fables were "always esteemed the best lessons for youth, as being well adapted to convey the most useful maxims, in an agreeable manner," most early editions of Aesop's work were priced beyond the means of parents of middling income. Moreover, although editors both anticipated and followed Locke in urging the benefits of reading Aesop, they did not bait their books with concessions to childhood. At last, in 1744, John Newbery published *A Little Pretty Pocket-Book, Intended for the Instruction and Amusement of Little Master Tommy, and Pretty Miss Polly. With Two Letters from Jack the Giant-Killer; As Also a Ball and Pincushion; The Use of which will infallibly make Tommy a good Boy, and Polly a good Girl.* The *Pocket-Book* was priced at six pence and written expressly for children. If Newbery did not "invent" children's books—and he came close—he showed that publishing for children could be profitable. By the end of the century, the trade in children's books was booming. As the title of *A Little Pretty Pocket-Book* shows, Newbery followed Locke closely, baiting instruction with amusement and appealing, in Locke's words, to children's delight in change and variety.

In 1757 Newbery published *Fables in Verse for the Improvement of the Young and the Old. By Abraham Aesop, Esq; To which are added, Fables in Verse and Prose, with the Conversation of Birds and Beasts, at their Several Meetings, Routs, and Assemblies. By Woglog, the Great Giant: Illustrated with a Variety of*

*Curious Cuts, by the Best Masters.* Also sold for six pence, the book was a typical Newbery miscellany, but one that pushed Aesop firmly into the nursery. In the preface Newbery defended fables and mixing amusement with instruction. People who read the book would discover, Newbery wrote, practically paraphrasing Locke, that "under agreeable allegories" children had been given "such lessons in prudence and morality, as may be of service to them in their riper years, and help to conduce them through the world with peace and tranquility." Like exercise, he argued, reading became tedious and painful if used only for "improvement in virtue." In contrast, "the virtue and instruction" got from a fable was like health got by hunting. Engaged in an agreeable pursuit, children became "insensible of the fatigues" with which it was "attended."

" 'Tis the very essence of a fable," Dodsley wrote, "to convey some moral or useful truth beneath the shadow of an allegory." At the end of the eighteenth century, moral critics attacked fiction and fairy tales, arguing that, by inflaming the imagination, fiction undermined judgment. Although Rousseau banished fables from the presence of Emilius, saying that the "charms of falsehood" so seduced children that they did not notice truths "crouched underneath" stories and thus were led more to "vice than to virtue," fables generally escaped criticism. Occasionally fables were identified with Christ's parables. When one character attacks fiction in David Fordyce's *Dialogues Concerning Education* (1745), another responds "that the Parabolical or Allegorical Way of instructing Mankind is vindicated by good Authority." "If not fables," he asks, what were "our Saviour's Parables?" For another eighteenth-century author, there was but "one accusation against Fables, namely Falsehood." This, Ellenor Fenn wrote, could be explained away by telling children that fables partook of "their favorite sport of making believe." Since fables were "generally pleasing to children" and could be used to "convey simple Morals adapted to the duties of childhood," "debating whether or no Fable-writing" was "the most desirable mode of instruction" wasted valuable educational time. In the 1780s, John Marshall began publishing books for children, many of the volumes, in contrast to those of Newbery, in big type and written in "infantine prattle" suited "to the gradual program of the young scholar." On Marshall's list in the mid-1780s were two of Ellenor Fenn's adaptations of Aesop, *Fables in Monosyllables by Mrs. Teachwell; To Which Are Added Morals in Dialogues, Between a Mother and Children* and *Fables by Mrs. Teachwell: In Which the Morals Are Drawn Incidentally in Various Ways.* "The want of proper books of instruction," the *Monthly Review* stated in 1784, was now supplied as "much laudable pains" had been taken to "furnish children with lessons of instruction in the agreeable forms of tales, fables, and historical anecdotes."

By the end of the eighteenth century, Aesop had become an almost universally approved children's author. Escaping criticism applied to other children's stories, namely that fictional narratives led the young astray by appealing to their imaginations, the fables became a staple of houses publishing books for children. This is not to say that adults stopped reading the fables. Newbery's nephew Francis published a three-penny "Carefully Revised and Improved" edition of Croxall's version sometime in the 1760s. The book appears to have been published for both adults and children and by 1788 reached a fourteenth edition. Nevertheless, during the nineteenth century, Aesop became so closely identified with children and the market for children's books that it is now difficult to think of the fables as adult reading.

Critics have long subjected the fables to interpretation, attaching explanations and instructive morals to the ends of fables almost as footnotes. In some instances remarks about individual fables were longer than the fables themselves. "Commentators," as the old rhyme puts it, "sometimes view/In Homer, more than Homer knew." For the most part, today's morals are epigrammatic. Ideas reflect their surroundings. Each age, indeed almost every editor, interprets Aesop differently. In part because no interpretation can be absolutely correct, the fables have not been imprisoned in truth. Consequently they have remained vital and capable of provoking thought. Many tales that appealed to the eighteenth-century audience, for example, might repulse a modern reader nurtured on the English Romantic poets and their sentimental celebration of imagination and individuality.

Indeed, today many fables seem inordinately cautionary, warning readers against imagination and urging them to be satisfied with their stations in life. If childhood reading really determined the course of living, and generations suckled on Aesop matured into frugal adults satisfied by simplicity, capitalism would have vanished. Despite "The Woman and the Fat Hen," "The Goose with the Golden Eggs," and "The Dog and the Shadow," among other fables, greed or the desire to better one's material lot does oil the wheels of progress. Countless tales preach about being satisfied with one's lot, offering a sort of consolation to the downtrodden. For example, "The Oak and the Reed" implies that position and strength may not be blessings, much as the Beatitudes offer consolation to the poor in spirit. In the future, when death uproots the oak, the lowly reed may inherit the kingdom of heaven. No matter how bad one's circumstances, "The Hares and the Frogs" teaches, you should be satisfied because someone else is worse off. Don't try to change the government, for any future government is liable to be worse than the present one, implies "The Hawk and the Pigeons" and "The Frogs Who Desired a

King." Such "messages" are conservative and perpetuate the status quo ante.

Other fables urge readers to be satisfied with themselves as they are ("The Monkey and the Camel" and "The Vain Crow"). But living involves change. One eats the apple, is kicked out of Eden, and learns. "Know thyself" should satisfy no one. "Know thy selves" would be better. Life may be real and earnest, as Longfellow put it, but it can also be fun. If the tortoise in "The Tortoise and the Eagle" had not become dissatisfied with his low station, he might have lived to a cynical, diseased old age. Today we favor self-improvement: "Be all you can be"; don't sink into comfortable, safe dissatisfaction and a life of decent resignation.

Modern Westerners are Lockeans, whether they realize it or not. Affluence has given people opportunities that did not exist in the past. Instead of being true to a single self, many people are wealthy enough to believe that they can shape new selves, especially with the help of education. The heroes and heroines of many contemporary children's books did not study the fables closely. They are not, in Wordsworth's words, model children educated into self-serving caution but "bad" boys and girls. Often such characters are disobedient and uneducated, indeed frequently so uneducable they become the voices of natural truth and decency. Some examples are Sissy Jupe in Dickens's *Hard Times* and Huck Finn, who because he isn't learned or "good" chooses not to betray the slave Jim, uttering perhaps the most "American" line in nineteenth-century literature, "All right, then, I'll *go* to hell."

The world is frightful, and in prescribing Aesop, educators and parents attempted to inoculate young readers against the unknown, at least for the first vulnerable years of children's lives. Frailty, thy name may be both living and not living. At times the fables are so cautionary that they isolate, implying life is so dangerous that only wary anchorites will survive. Don't trust those who appear to be friends ("The Wolf and the Shepherd"). Beware genuine friendship ("The Sick Stag"). Do not wish for talents that expose you to public view ("The Fir Tree and the Bramble"). Don't listen to people ("The Miller, His Son, and Their Ass"). Beware tricksters and distrust everyone, even those who appear ill ("The Sick Lion"). Don't be a Good Samaritan ("The Wolf and the Sheep" and "The Farmer and the Snake").

Although readers may delight in the fables and their illustrations, the fables rarely celebrate the imaginative or the spontaneous and sensual. (See "The Astronomer" and "The Maid and the Pail of Milk.") For me one of the shortcomings of the fables is the failure to appreciate creativity. If one reads "The Shepherd Boy and the Wolf," with its famous little boy crying wolf, not as a tale warning children against lying, but as being about creativity, then the meaning shifts radically. What happens to the imagination if people never cry wolf or don't stray from conventional behavior, be, thier behavior literary or political? What would people's lives be if they ignored the sweets of existence—flowers, caterpillars, warm days, all the beauty of this glorious life—as suggested by "The Flies and the Honey Jar"? One of the most famous of Aesop's fables is "The Ants and the Grasshopper." Do parents really want children to become corporate ants? How much better to be a grasshopper, bringing song into the world, if only for a season. What makes life better: more anthills or lines like "thick as Autumnal Leaves that strow the Brooks/In Vallombrosa"?

Among other famous fables is the "The Hare and the Tortoise," in which the hardworking tortoise triumphs over the lazy, irresponsible hare. The story smacks of inspirational sayings posted in high school locker rooms, maxims such as "It's not the size of the dog in the fight that counts, but the size of the fight in the dog" and "When the going gets tough, the tough get going." Indeed, it anticipates *The Little Engine That Could*, a wonderful story but one adults know is fiction. Big dogs turn little dogs into lunch. When the going gets tough, the smart go somewhere else—to America perhaps. Saying "I think I can" won't pull a big train over a mountain, no matter how intensely people want to believe that it is possible. In most of the world, the tortoise represents the ordinary person, the oppressed underdog, the child threatened by ogrelike adults. Outside of Aesop, the tortoise wins the race by using trickery or, metaphorically, his intelligence. See "Mr. Rabbit Finds His Match at Last" in *Uncle Remus: His Songs and His Sayings.*

Happily, all selections of fables are inconsistent. The implication of a fable on one page clashes with that of a fable on the next page. In contrast to "The Farmer and the Snake," "The Lion and the Mouse" rewards the Good Samaritan. Instead of suggesting that one should retire meekly from life and deed to isolated safety, "The Boy and the Nettle" urges readers to act decisively. Other fables eschew isolation and teach the good lesson that people inhabit a social world in which the happiness of others affects their own well-being, or as "The Belly and the Members" might put it, "No pancreas is an organ entire of itself." Surely devotees of Thoreau must like "The Country Mouse and the Town Mouse." "The Crow and the Pitcher" appeals to planners of all sorts, ranging from the urban to the pedagogical. As for me, whenever a youngster naïve with certainty says he knows how to solve some complex problem, I nod and think of "The Mice in Council" and belling that cat. Time also changes one's perspective. Instead of being "a miserable cur," the canine protagonist of "The Dog in the Manger" now strikes me as understandable. He is not thoughtless; he is just old and grumpy—big-bellied and sore-headed, a bit like Aesop after life tossed him from the rock above Delos.

—Sam Pickering

# I

# The Fox and the Grapes

A famished fox crept into a vineyard where ripe, luscious grapes were draped high upon arbors in a most tempting display. In his effort to win a juicy prize, the fox jumped and sprang many times but failed in all his attempts. When he finally had to admit defeat, he retreated and muttered to himself, "Well, what does it matter anyway? The grapes are sour!"

*It is easy to despise what you cannot get.*

# II

## The Wolf and the Crane

A wolf devoured his prey so ravenously that a bone got stuck in his throat, and in extreme agony, he ran and howled throughout the forest, beseeching every animal he met to pull out the bone. He even offered a generous reward to anyone who succeeded in pulling it out. Moved by his pleas as well as the prospect of the money, a crane ventured her long neck down the wolf's throat and drew out the bone. She then modestly asked for the promised reward, but the wolf just grinned and bared his teeth.

"Ungrateful creature!" he replied with seeming indignation. "How dare you ask for any other reward than your life? After all, you're among the very few who can say that you've put your head into the jaws of a wolf and were permitted to draw it out in safety."

*Expect no reward when you serve the wicked, and be thankful if you escape injury for your pains.*

# III

## The Archer and the Lion

An archer, known for his skill with bow and arrow, went to the mountains in search of game. When he entered the wilderness, all the beasts of the forest became terrified and took flight. Only the lion challenged him to combat, whereupon the archer immediately launched an arrow and cried out, "My messenger has something to say to you!"

The lion was wounded in the side, and smarting with pain, he fled deep into the thickets. When a fox saw him running away, however, he encouraged him to turn and face his enemy.

"No," said the lion, "there's no way you can persuade me to fight. Just think, if a mere messenger can do as much damage as he's already done, how shall I withstand the attack of the man who sent him?"

*It is not a very pleasant feeling to have a neighbor who can easily strike from a distance.*

# IV

# The Woman and the Fat Hen

A woman owned a hen that laid an egg every morning. Since the hen's eggs were of excellent quality, they sold for a good price. So, at one point, the woman thought to herself, "If I double my hen's allowance of barley, she'll lay twice a day." Therefore, she put her plan to work, and the hen became so fat and contented that it stopped laying altogether.

*Relying on statistics does not always produce results.*

# V

## The Kid and the Wolf

Standing securely on a high rock, a kid noticed a wolf passing below and began to taunt him and shower him with abuse. The wolf merely stopped to reply, "Coward! Don't think that you can annoy me. As far as I'm concerned, it's not you who's taunting me, but the place on which you're standing!"

## VI

# The Hawk and the Pigeons

Some pigeons had long lived in fear of a hawk, but since they had always kept on the alert and stayed near their dovecote, they had consistently managed to escape their enemy's attacks. Finding his sallies unsuccessful, the hawk now sought to use cunning to trick the pigeons.

"Why," he once asked, "do you prefer this life of constant anxiety when I could keep you safe from any conceivable attack by the kites and falcons? All you have to do is to make me your king, and I won't bother you anymore."

Trusting his claims, the pigeons elected him to their throne, but no sooner was he installed than he began exercising his royal prerogative by devouring a pigeon a day.

"It serves us right," said one poor pigeon whose turn was yet to come.

*Some remedies are worse than the disease itself.*

# VII

## The Eagle and the Fox

An eagle and a fox had lived together for a long time as good neighbors. The eagle's nest was on top of a high tree; the fox's lair, at the foot of it. One day, however, while the fox was away, the eagle could not find any food for her young ones. So she swooped down and carried off one of the fox's cubs to her nest, thinking that her lofty dwelling would protect her from the fox's revenge. She was about to divide the cub among her brood, when the fox returned home and pleaded fervently for the return of her young cub. Since her entreaties were in vain, she ran to an altar in a neighboring field and snatched a torch from the fire that had been lit to sacrifice a goat. Then she returned to the tree and set it on fire. The flames and smoke soon caused the eagle to worry about her young ones and her own life as well, and she returned the cub safe and sound to his mother.

*The tyrant is never safe from those whom he oppresses.*

# VIII

# The Boy and the Scorpion

A boy was hunting locusts on a wall and had already caught a great number of them when he spied a scorpion and mistook it for another locust. Just as he was cupping his hand to catch it, the scorpion lifted up its sting and said, "Just you try, and you'll not only lose me but all your locusts in the bargain!"

# IX

# The Fox and the Goat

A fox had fallen into a well and could not find any means to escape. Eventually, a thirsty goat appeared, and upon noticing the fox, he asked him whether the water was good and plentiful.

Pretending that his situation was not precarious, the fox replied, "Come down, my friend. The water is so good that I can't drink enough of it. Besides, there's such an abundant supply that it can't be exhausted."

When he heard this, the goat did not waste any time and promptly leaped down into the well. After he quenched his thirst, the fox informed him of their predicament and suggested a scheme for their common escape.

"If you will place your forefeet upon the wall and bend your head, I'll run up your back and escape. Then I'll help you out."

The goat readily agreed to this proposal, and the fox took advantage of his friend's back and horns and nimbly propelled himself out of the well. Following his escape, he made off as fast as he could, while the goat yelled and reproached him for breaking their bargain. But the fox turned around and coolly remarked to the poor deluded goat, "If you had half as much brains as you have beard, you would never have gone down the well before making sure there was a way up. I'm sorry that I can't stay with you any longer, but I have some business that needs my attention."

*Look before you leap.*

# X

## The Old Hound

An old hound had served his master extremely well in the field but had lost his strength over the years and now had many troubles. One day, while out hunting with his master, he encountered a wild boar and boldly seized the beast by the ear, but his teeth gave way, and the boar escaped. His master rushed to the scene and began giving the hound a good scolding and sound beating, but he stopped when the feeble dog looked up and said, "Spare your old servant, dear master! You know full well that neither my courage nor my will were at fault, but only my strength and my teeth, and these I have lost in your service."

# XI

## The Ants and the Grasshopper

On a cold, frosty day the ants began dragging out some of the grain they had stored during the summer and began drying it. A grasshopper, half-dead with hunger, came by and asked the ants for a morsel to save his life.

"What did you do this past summer?" responded the ants.

"Oh," said the grasshopper, "I kept myself busy by singing all day long and all night, too."

"Well then," remarked the ants, as they laughed and shut their storehouse, "since you kept yourself busy by singing all summer, you can do the same by dancing all winter."

*Idleness brings want.*

# XII

# The Fawn and Her Mother

One day a fawn said to her mother, "You're larger than a dog and swifter. You also have greater endurance and horns to defend yourself. Why is it then, Mother, that you're so afraid of the hounds?"

She smiled and said, "I know all this full well, my child. But no sooner do I hear a dog bark than I feel faint and take off as fast as my heels can carry me."

*No argument, no matter how convincing, will give courage to a coward.*

# XIII

# The Horse and the Groom

A dishonest groom used to steal and sell a horse's oats and grain on a regular basis. He would, however, spend hours busily grooming and rubbing him down to make him appear in good condition. Naturally the horse resented this treatment and said, "If you really want me to look well, groom me less, and feed me more."

# XIV

# The Mountain in Labor

Many years ago a mighty rumbling was heard from a mountain, which was said to be in labor. Thousands of people flocked from far and near to see what it would produce. After a long time of waiting in anxious expectation—out popped a mouse!

*A magnificent and promising beginning often ends in a paltry performance.*

# XV

## The Flies and the Honey Jar

After a jar of honey was knocked over in a kitchen, the flies were attracted by its sweet smell and began eating the honey. Indeed, they swarmed all over it and did not budge from the spot until they had devoured every drop. However, their feet had become so clogged that they could not fly away, no matter how much they tried. Stymied by their own voracious appetites, they cried out, "What foolish creatures we are! We've thrown away our lives just for the sake of a little pleasure."

# XVI

# The Two Bags

According to ancient lore, every man is born into the world with two bags suspended from his neck—one in front and one behind, and both are full of faults. But the one in front is full of his neighbor's faults; the one behind, full of his own. Consequently, men are blind to their own faults but never lose sight of their neighbor's.

LE VOLEUR

# XVII

# The Vain Crow

A crow, as vain and conceited as only a crow can be, picked up the feathers that some peacocks had shed and stuck them among his own. Then he scoffed at his old companions and joined a flock of beautiful peacocks. After introducing himself with great self-confidence, the crow was immediately recognized for the intruder he was, and the peacocks stripped him of his borrowed plumes. Moreover, they battered him with their beaks and sent him about his business. The unlucky crow, sorely punished and deeply regretful, rejoined his former companions and wanted to mix with them again as if nothing had happened. But they recalled the airs he had assumed and drove him from their flock. At the same time, one of the crows whom he had recently snubbed gave him this short lecture: "Had you been satisfied with your own feathers, you would have escaped the punishment of your betters, and also the contempt of your equals."

# XVIII

# The Wolf and the Lamb

While lapping water at the head of a running brook, a wolf noticed a stray lamb some distance down the stream. Once he made up his mind to attack her, he began thinking of a plausible excuse for making her his prey.

"Scoundrel!" he cried, running up to her. "How dare you muddle the water that I am drinking!"

"Please forgive me," replied the lamb meekly, "but I don't see how I could have done anything to the water since it runs from you to me, not from me to you."

"Be that as it may," the wolf retorted, "but you know it was only a year ago that you called me many bad names behind my back."

"Oh, sir," said the lamb, "I wasn't even born a year ago."

"Well," the wolf asserted, "if it wasn't you, it was your mother, and that's all the same to me. Anyway, it's no use trying to argue me out of my supper."

And without another word, he fell upon the poor helpless lamb and tore her to pieces.

*A tyrant will always find a pretext for his tyranny. So it is useless for the innocent to seek justice through reasoning when the oppressor intends to be unjust.*

# XIX

## The Bear and the Fox

A bear used to boast of his excessive love for humankind, saying that he never touched or mauled a human corpse.

The fox observed with a smile, "I would be more impressed by your kindness if you never ate a human being alive."

*We should not wait until a person dies before showing our respect.*

# XX

# The Dog, the Cock, and the Fox

A dog and a cock set out on their travels together, and by nightfall they found themselves in a forest. So the cock flew up into a tree and perched himself on a high branch, while the dog dozed below at the foot. When day finally dawned, the cock, as usual, crowed very loudly and drew the attention of a fox, who thought he would make a meal out of him. So he approached the tree and spoke to the cock from beneath the branches: "You're such a good little bird and most useful to your fellow creatures. So, why don't you come down, and we can sing our matins and rejoice together?"

"Go to the foot of the tree, my good friend," replied the cock, "and tell my sacristan to toll the bell."

But when the fox approached the foot of the tree, the dog promptly jumped up and made a quick end of him.

*He who lays traps for others is often caught by his own snare.*

# XXI

# The Cock and the Jewel

A cock was scratching the ground in a farmyard in search of food for himself and his hens, when he happened to turn up a jewel. Feeling quite sure that it was something precious, but not knowing exactly what to do with it, he remarked, "You're undoubtedly a very fine thing for those who appreciate your worth. But I'd rather have one grain of delicious barley than all the jewels in the world."

*The value of an object is in the eyes of the beholder.*

# XXII

# The Sea Gull and the Hawk

A sea gull, who was more at home swimming on the sea than walking on land, liked to catch live fish for its food. One day the gull pounced upon a fish, and as he tried to swallow it, he choked, burst a gullet, and lay down on the shore to die. A hawk, who was passing by and saw him, thought he was a land bird like himself. Consequently, he offered him no other comfort than, "It serves you right! What business is it of birds of the air to seek food from the sea?"

# XXIII

## The Fox and the Lion

A fox had never seen a lion before, and when he finally encountered one for the first time, he was so terrified that he almost died of fright. When he met him the second time, he was still afraid but managed to conceal his fear. When he saw him the third time, he was so emboldened that he went up to him and began having a familiar conversation with him.

*Familiarity breeds contempt.*

# XXIV

## The Creaking Wheels

As some oxen were pulling a wagon along a bumpy road, the wheels began to creak and make a tremendous noise, whereupon the driver cried to the wagon, "Brute! Why do you groan when those creatures who are doing all the work are silent?"

*Those who cry the loudest are not always the ones who are hurt the most.*

# XXV

# The Frog and the Ox

An ox was grazing in a swampy meadow when he accidentally set his foot down on top of a bunch of young frogs and crushed nearly all of them to death. One that managed to escape ran off to tell his mother the dreadful news.

"Mother," he said, "it was a beast, a big four-footed beast, that did it!"

The mother, who was a vain old thing, thought she could easily make herself as large. "How big? Was it as big as this?" she asked and puffed herself as much as she could.

"Oh," said the little one, "a great deal bigger than that!"

"Well, was it this big?" she cried, puffing and blowing again with all her might.

"It certainly was, Mother," he replied, "and I'm afraid you'd probably burst before you could reach even half its size."

Provoked by such a disparagement of her powers, the silly old frog made one more try before she did indeed succeed in bursting herself into thin air.

*Not all creatures can become as great as they think.*

# XXVI

## The Farmer and the Snake

Returning home one winter's day, a farmer found a snake lying under a hedge, half dead with cold. Taking pity on the creature, he placed it in his bosom and brought it home, where he laid it upon the hearth near the fire. No sooner was the snake restored by the warmth of the cottage than it began to attack the farmer's wife and children. Hearing their cries, the farmer, whose compassion had saved the snake's life, rushed into the room, grabbed an ax, and smashed the serpent until it was dead.

*Kindness to ungrateful and vicious creatures is thrown away.*

# XXVII

# The Lion and the Fox

A fox agreed to work for a lion as a servant, and for a while, each carried out his respective duties according to his own nature and powers. The fox used to point out the prey, and the lion would attack and seize it. The fox, however, soon became jealous of the lion for carrying off the lion's share. Thinking that he was just as good as his master, the fox declared that he would no longer simply discover the prey but capture it on his own. The next day, just as he was about to snatch a lamb from the fold, the hunter and his hounds appeared and made him their prize for the day.

*Keep your place in life, and your place will keep you.*

# XXVIII

## The Fisherman and His Music

A man who cared more for music than his nets saw some fish in the sea and began playing on his flute. He thought they would jump out on shore and hop into his net, but he was disappointed when he found that the fish would not comply. So he decided to cast his net and snared a great number of them. After he pulled them to shore, the fish began to dance and flap, but he said, "Since you wouldn't dance when I piped, I'll have none of your dancing now."

*It takes great skill to do the right thing at the right time.*

# XXIX

# The Domesticated Dog and the Wolf

A lean, hungry wolf happened to meet a plump, well-fed dog one bright moonlit night. After the first compliments were exchanged, the wolf asked, "How is it, my friend, that you look so sleek? Your food certainly agrees with you while I must struggle for my living day and night and can hardly keep myself from starving!"

"Well," replied the dog, "if you want to live as well as I do, you only have to act the way I do."

"And how is that?" countered the wolf.

"You only have to guard the master's house," said the dog, "and keep the thieves away at night."

"It will be my pleasure," the wolf responded. "I've been going through a bad time. Life in the woods is hard work for me because of the frost and rain. To have a warm roof over my head and a bellyful of food always at my disposal will be, I think, worth the change."

"Well," said the dog, "all you have to do is follow me."

As they began jogging along together, the wolf noticed a mark on the dog's neck and, since he was curious, he could not keep himself from asking how it got there.

"Pooh!" remarked the dog. "It's nothing."

"Well, then, tell me," insisted the wolf.

"Oh, it's a mere trifle," said the dog. "It probably got there from the collar that's fastened to my chain."

"Chain!" the wolf cried in surprise. "Do you mean to say that you can't rove whenever and wherever you want?"

"Not exactly," the dog said. "You see, I'm regarded as rather fierce. So, sometimes they tie me up during the day, but I assure you that I'm perfectly free to go where I want at night, and the master feeds me off his own plate, and the servants give me their tidbits. I tell you, I'm such a favorite, and—but what's the matter? Where are you going?"

"Farewell, my friend," said the wolf. "You're welcome to your dainties, but for me, a dry crust with liberty will always be worth more than all the luxury a king with a chain could ever provide."

# XXX

# The Country Mouse and the Town Mouse

Once upon a time a country mouse, who had a friend in town, invited him to pay a visit in the country for old acquaintance's sake. After the invitation was accepted, the country mouse, though plain, coarse, and somewhat frugal, opened his heart and pantry to honor his old friend and to show him the proper hospitality. There was not a morsel which he had carefully stored that he did not bring forth out of its larder—peas and barley, cheese parings and nuts—with the hope that the quantity would make up for what he feared was wanting in quality to suit the taste of his elegant guest. In turn, the town mouse condescended to nibble a little here and there in a dainty manner while the host sat munching a blade of barley straw. In their after-dinner chat the town mouse said to the country mouse, "How is it, my good friend, that you can endure this boring and crude life? You live like a toad in a hole. You can't really prefer these solitary rocks and woods to streets teeming with carriages and people. Upon my word of honor, you're wasting your time in such a miserable existence. You must make the most of your life while it lasts. As you know, a mouse does not live forever. So, come with me this very night, and I'll show you all around the town and what life's about."

Overcome by his friend's fine words and polished

manner, the country mouse agreed, and they set out together on their journey to the town. It was late in the evening when they crept stealthily into the city and midnight before they reached the large house, which was the town mouse's residence. There were couches of crimson velvet, ivory carvings, and everything one could imagine that indicated wealth and luxury. On the table were the remains of a splendid banquet from all the choicest shops ransacked the day before to make sure that the guests, already departed, would be satisfied. It was now the town mouse's turn to play host, and he placed his country friend on a purple cushion, ran back and forth to supply all his needs, and pressed dish upon dish on him and delicacy upon delicacy. Of course, the town mouse tasted each and every course before he ventured to place it before his rustic cousin, as though he were waiting on a king. In turn, the country mouse made himself quite at home and blessed the good fortune that had brought about such a change in his way of life. In the middle of his enjoyment, however, just as he was thinking contemptuously of the poor meals that he had been accustomed to eating, the door suddenly flew open, and a group of revelers, who were returning from a late party, burst into the room. The frightened friends jumped from the table and hid themselves in the very first corner they could reach. No sooner did they dare creep out again than the barking of dogs drove them back with even greater terror than before. Gradually, when things seemed quiet, the country mouse crept out from his hiding place and whispered good-bye to his elegant friend.

"This fine mode of living may be all right for those who like it," he said. "But I'd rather have a crust in peace and safety than all your fine things in the midst of such alarm and terror."

# XXXI

## The Dog and the Shadow

A dog had stolen a piece of meat out of a butcher shop and was crossing a river on his way home when he saw his own shadow reflected in the water below. Thinking that it was another dog with another piece of meat, he became intent on capturing the other piece as well. Once he snapped at the treasure below, however, he dropped the prize that he was carrying and thus lost everything he had.

*Grasp at the shadow and you will lose the substance.*

# XXXII

# The Moon and Her Mother

The moon once asked her mother to make her a little cloak that would fit her well.

"How can I make a cloak to fit you?" her mother asked. "Right now you're a new moon, but soon you'll turn into a full moon, and later you'll become neither one nor the other."

# XXXIII

# The Fighting Cocks and the Eagle

Two young cocks were fighting fiercely for the right to rule a dunghill. At last, the one who was beaten crept into the corner of the hen house, covered with wounds. The victor flew straight to the top of an outhouse, clapped his wings, and crowed loudly to announce his victory. Just then an eagle swooped down from the sky, grabbed him with his talons, and carried him away. After watching all this from his hiding place, the defeated rival came out, took possession of the dunghill, and strutted about among his hens with all the dignity of a majestic king.

*Pride goes before defeat.*

# XXXIV

# The Man and the Satyr

After a man and a satyr became friends, they began talking together. Since it was a cold wintry day, the man put his fingers to his mouth and blew on them.

"Why are you doing that, my friend?" the satyr asked.

"To warm my hands," said the man. "They're nearly frozen."

Later on in the day, they sat down to eat. Some hot food was placed before them, and the man raised the dish to his mouth and blew on it.

"And what's that for?" asked the satyr.

"Oh," replied the man, "my porridge is so hot that I need to cool it off."

"Well, then," said the satyr, "from this moment on, you can consider our friendship terminated. I could never trust anyone who blows hot one moment and cold the next."

# XXXV

## The Tortoise and the Eagle

A tortoise was dissatisfied with his lowly life and with crawling about on the ground at a snail's pace. He envied the birds, who could soar high into the clouds whenever they desired. He thought that, if he could but once get up into the air, he would be able to fly with the best of them. So, one day he offered an eagle all the treasures in the ocean if he would only teach him how to fly. The eagle declined and assured him that the tortoise's desire to fly was not only absurd but impossible. However, the tortoise kept insisting and pleading so that the eagle eventually agreed to do the best he could for him. Therefore, he carried the tortoise high up in the air, and as he let go of him, he said, "Now, spread your legs!" But before the tortoise could say one word to him in response, he plunged straight down, hit a rock, and was dashed to pieces.

*Demand your own way, demand your own ruin.*

# XXXVI

# The Mule

A mule had grown fat and wanton from his huge daily rations of corn, and one day, as he was jumping, kicking, and gamboling about the fields, he thought to himself, "My mother must surely have been a thoroughbred racer, and I'm quite as good as she ever was!"

But he was soon exhausted from the galloping and frisking, and all at once he remembered that his sire had been nothing but an ass.

*Every truth has two sides. It is best to look at both before we declare where we stand.*

# XXXVII

# The Hen and the Cat

Hearing that a hen was laid up sick in her nest, a cat paid a visit out of sympathy. After creeping up to her, he said, "How are you, my dear friend? What can I do for you? Do you need anything? Just tell me, and I'll bring you anything in the world you want. Just keep up your spirits, and don't be alarmed."

"Thank you," said the hen. "Just be good enough to leave me, and I'm sure that I'll soon get well again."

*Uninvited guests are often most welcome when they leave.*

## XXXVIII

# The Old Woman and the Wine Bottle

An old woman found an empty wine bottle that had once been filled with choice wine and still retained the fragrant smell of its former contents. Though not a drop of the choice wine remained, the old woman pressed her nose to the top of the bottle as close as she could, and after sniffing with all her might, she exclaimed, "Sweet creature! How good your contents must have been when the dregs are still so delicious!"

# XXXIX

# The Hare and the Tortoise

A hare once ridiculed the short feet and slow pace of the tortoise. But the tortoise laughed and replied, "Though you may be as swift as the wind, I'll beat you in a race."

"All right," said the hare, "you'll soon live to regret those words."

So they agreed that the fox would choose the course and fix the goal. On the day appointed for the race, the tortoise started crawling at his usual steady pace without stopping a solitary moment. Of course, the hare soon left the tortoise far behind. Once he reached the midway mark, he began to nibble some juicy grass and amuse himself in different ways. Since the day was warm, he thought he would take a little nap in a shady spot. Even if the tortoise might pass him while he slept, he was confident that he could easily overtake him again before he reached the goal. Meanwhile, the unwavering tortoise plodded on straight toward the goal. When the hare finally awoke, he was surprised to find that the tortoise was nowhere to be seen, and headed for the finish line as fast as he could. However, he dashed across the line only to see that the tortoise had crossed it before him and was comfortably resting and waiting for his arrival.

*Slow and steady wins the race.*

## XL

# The Ass and the Grasshopper

After hearing some grasshoppers chirping, an ass was enchanted by their music and wanted to acquire the same melodic charms. When he asked them what they ate to sing so sweetly, they told him that they dined on nothing but dew. Consequently, the ass followed the same diet, but he soon died of hunger.

*One man's meat is another man's poison.*

# XLI

# The Lamb and the Wolf

Pursued by a wolf, a lamb took refuge in a temple. When the wolf cried out to the lamb that the priest would slay him if he caught him, the lamb responded, "So be it. I'd rather be sacrificed in the temple than be devoured by you!"

# XLII

# The Crab and Its Mother

"Why do you walk so crooked, child?" said an old crab to her young one. "Walk straight!"

"Mother," the young crab replied, "show me the way, and when I see you moving straight ahead, I'll try to follow."

*Actions speak louder than words.*

# XLIII

## Jupiter and the Camel

Hundreds of years ago, the camel asked Jupiter to grant him horns because he felt deprived and defenseless when he regarded other animals.

"The bull," said he, "has horns, the boar, tusks, and the lion and tiger, sharp claws and fangs that make them feared and respected everywhere. On the other hand, I have to put up with the abuse of all those who insult me."

Jupiter angrily responded that, if he would take the trouble to think, he would see that he was endowed with his own unique qualities. So, not only did Jupiter refuse to give the camel horns, but he also cropped his ears short for being so impudent.

*By asking for too much, we may lose the little that we once had.*

# XLIV

## The Mouse and the Frog

On an ill-fated day a mouse made the acquaintance of a frog, and they set off on their travels together. The frog pretended to be very fond of the mouse and invited him to visit the pond in which he lived. To keep his companion out of harm's way, the frog tied the mouse's front foot to his own hind leg, and thus they proceeded for some distance by land. When they came to the pond, the frog told the mouse to trust him and be brave as he began swimming across the water. But, no sooner had they reached the middle of the pond than the frog suddenly plunged to the bottom, dragging the unfortunate mouse after him. Now the struggling and floundering mouse made such a great commotion in the water that he managed to attract the attention of a hawk, who pounced upon the mouse and carried him away to be devoured. Since the frog was still tied to the mouse, he shared the same fate of his companion and was justly punished for his treachery.

*Whoever plots the downfall of his neighbor is often betrayed by his own treachery.*

# XLV

## The Shepherd Boy and the Wolf

A shepherd boy, who tended his flock not far from a village, used to amuse himself at times by crying out "Wolf! Wolf!" His trick succeeded two or three times, and the whole village came running to his rescue. However, the villagers were simply rewarded with laughter for their pains.

One day the wolf really did come, and the boy cried out in earnest. But his neighbors thought that he was up to his old tricks and paid no attention to his cries. Consequently, the sheep were left at the mercy of the wolf.

*Even when liars tell the truth, they are never believed.*

# XLVI

## The Peach, the Apple, and the Blackberry

The peach and the apple decided to have a contest to determine which one was more beautiful than the other. However, when tempers flared and the competition appeared to be getting out of hand, a blackberry thrust his head from a nearby bush and cried out, "This dispute's gone on long enough. Let's all be friends and stop this nonsense!"

*The loudest quarrels are often the most petty.*

# XLVII

# The Hare and the Hound

A hound scared a hare from a bush and chased him for some distance, but the hare was faster and got away. A goatherd, who happened to pass by at the time, mocked the hound for letting a scrawny hare outrun him.

"You forget," replied the hound, "that it's one thing to run for your dinner and another to run for your life."

# XLVIII

# The Stag in the Ox Stall

Hard pressed by the hounds, a stag was driven out of his cover and bolted in terror over the fields. Blind through fear, he took refuge in a farmyard and hid himself in an ox stall, which happened to be open. As he was trying to conceal himself under some straw, an ox asked, "Don't you know that it's certain death if you stay here?"

"Just don't betray me," said the stag, "and I'll be off again at my first opportunity."

Toward evening the herdsman came to feed the cattle, but did not notice the stag. The other farm servants came in and out of the barn, and the stag remained safe. Then, after the foreman passed though, everything seemed all right. So the stag now felt quite secure and began to thank the oxen for their silence and hospitality.

"Wait awhile," said one of them. "We really wish you well, but there's another person that may give you trouble, one with a hundred eyes. If he shou[illegible]en to come this way, I fear that your life will stiii [illegible] jeopardy."

While he was speaking, the master, having finished his supper, made the rounds to see that everything was safe for the night, for he thought that his cattle had not been looking as well as they should be. When he went up to the rack, he asked his servants, "Why is there so little fodder here? Why isn't there more straw?" Then he added, "I wonder how long it would take to sweep out those cobwebs?"

As he began prying and looking here, there, and everywhere, he caught sight of the stag's antlers jutting out from the straw, and he immediately called in his servants, who seized the poor beast.

*Nothing escapes the master's eye.*

# XLIX

# The Crow and the Pitcher

A crow, on the verge of dying with thirst, spied a pitcher in the distance and flew to it with joy. But when he arrived, he discovered to his grief it contained so little water that he could not possibly get at it, despite all his efforts. At one point he decided to turn the pitcher over and break it. However, he was not strong enough to succeed. At last, seeing some small pebbles nearby, he gathered them and dropped them into the pitcher one by one. By this means the water gradually rose to the brim, and he could quench his thirst with ease.

*Necessity is the mother of invention.*

# L

## The Lion and the Mouse

A lion was sleeping in his lair when a mouse mistakenly ran over the mighty beast's nose and awakened him. The lion grabbed the frightened little creature with his paw and was just about to crush him when the mouse began pleading for mercy and declared that he had not consciously intended to offend the lion. Moreover, the mouse sought to convince the lion not to stain his honorable paws with such an insignificant prey. Smiling at his little prisoner's fright, the lion generously let him go.

Now a short time after this occurrence the lion was caught in a net laid by some hunters while roaming the woods in search of prey. Finding himself entangled in rope without the hope of escape, the lion let out a roar that resounded throughout the entire forest. Recognizing the voice of his former savior, the mouse ran to the spot, and without much ado, began nibbling the knots that had ensnared the lion. In a short time he freed the noble beast and thus convinced him that kindness is seldom wasted and that, no matter how meager a creature may be, he may have it in his power to return a good deed.

*Little friends may prove great friends.*

# LI

## The One-Eyed Doe

A one-eyed doe used to graze near the sea, and in order to protect herself from attack, she kept her eye focused on the land in case hunters might approach, while her blind side was turned toward the sea because she did not expect a threat from that direction. But some sailors came rowing by in a boat, and when they saw her, they took aim from the water and shot her. Heaving her last gasp, she sighed, "Unfortunate creature that I am! I was safe on the land side where I expected to be attacked, but found an enemy in the sea to which I looked most for protection."

*Danger often comes from a source that is least suspected.*

# LII

# The Trees and the Ax

A woodsman went into the forest and petitioned the trees to provide him a handle for his ax. It seemed so modest a request that the principal trees granted it right away, and they declared that the plain homely ash should furnish what he needed. No sooner had the woodsman fitted the staff for his purpose, however, than he began chopping down the noblest trees in the woods. By the time the oak grasped the entire matter, it was too late, and he whispered to a neighboring cedar, "With our first concession we lost everything. If we had not sacrificed our humble neighbor, we might still be able to stand for ages."

*When the rich surrender the rights of the poor, they provide a handle to be used against their own privileges.*

# LIII

## The Lion, the Ass, and the Fox Who Went Hunting

One day the lion, the ass, and the fox went hunting together, and it was agreed that whatever they caught would be shared between them. After killing a large stag, they decided to have a hearty meal. The lion asked the ass to divide the spoils, and after the ass made three equal parts, he told his friends to take their pick, whereupon the lion, in great indignation, seized the ass and tore him to pieces. He then told the fox to divide the spoils, and the fox gathered everything into one great pile except for a tiny portion that he reserved for himself.

"Ah, friend," asked the lion, "who taught you to divide things so equally?"

"I needed no other lesson," replied the fox, "than the ass's fate."

*Better to learn from the mistakes of others than by your own.*

# LIV

## The Travelers and the Bear

Two friends were traveling on the same road together when they encountered a bear. Without thinking about his companion, one of the travelers, a nimble fellow, climbed up a tree in great fear and hid himself. The other realized that he had no chance to fight the bear single-handedly, so he threw himself on the ground and pretended to be dead, for he had heard that bears will never touch a dead body. As he lay there, the bear came up to his head, and sniffed his nose, ears, and heart, but the man remained still and held his breath. Finally, the bear was convinced that he was dead and walked away. When the bear was out of sight, the man in the tree came down and asked what it was that the bear had whispered to him, for he had observed that the bear had put his mouth close to his friend's ear.

"It was no great secret," the other replied. "He merely told me to watch out for the company I keep and not to trust people who abandon their friends in difficult times."

*Adversity tests the sincerity of friends.*

# LV

## The Belly and the Members

Long ago when the members of the human body had very strong wills of their own and did not work together as amicably as they do now, they denounced the belly for leading an idle and luxurious life, while they were wholly occupied in supporting it and ministering to its wants and pleasures. At one point, they agreed to cut off the belly's supplies for the future. The hands declared that they would not lift a thing, not even a crust of bread; the mouth that it would not accept any more food for the teeth to chew; the legs that they would no longer carry the belly from place to place, and so on with the others. No sooner did they set their plan of starving the belly into subjection than they all began, one by one, to fail and flag so that the whole body started to pine away. Consequently, the members became convinced that the belly, cumbersome and useless as it seemed to be, also had an important function of its own. In fact, they realized that they were just as dependent on it as it was on them and that if they wanted to keep the body in a healthy state, they would have to work together for the common good of all.

# LVI

## The Dolphins and the Sprat

The dolphins and the whales were at war with one another, and while the battle was at its height, the sprat stepped in and tried to separate them. But one of the dolphins cried out, "Let us alone! We'd rather die fighting than be reconciled by you."

# LVII

# The Blind Man and the Whelp

A blind man could distinguish any kind of animal simply by touching it. One time, some friends wanted to test him and brought him a wolf's whelp. After feeling it all over, the blind man was not entirely certain about the animal, and he said, "I'm not sure whether your father was a dog or a wolf, but I am certain about one thing: I would not trust you among a flock of sheep."

*Evil tendencies are shown early in life.*

# LVIII

## The Sick Stag

A stag whose joints had become stiff with old age fell sick and decided to lie down on the rich grass of a meadow close to some woods so that he might be able to graze more easily. Since he had always been a friendly and good neighbor, many beasts came to visit him and wish him farewell. Little by little, however, they began eating up all the grass until nothing was left. So, though the stag recovered from the disease, he had nothing to eat, and in the end, he died not so much from sickness or of old age as for sheer want of the food that his friends had eaten for him.

# LIX

# Hercules and the Wagoner

A farmer was carelessly driving his wagon along a muddy road when his wheels became stuck so deep in the clay that the horses came to a standstill. Consequently, the man dropped to his knees and began to pray for Hercules to come and help him without making the least effort to move the wagon himself. However, Hercules responded by telling him to lay his shoulder to the wheel and reminding him that heaven only aided those who tried to help themselves.

*Pray as we may, if we do not learn to help ourselves, all our prayers will go unheeded.*

# LX

# The Fox and the Woodcutter

A fox, who was hard pressed by some hounds during a hunt, approached a man who was cutting wood, and begged him to provide him with a hiding place. The man pointed to his own hut, and the fox crept inside and concealed himself in a corner. Soon the hunters arrived and asked the man whether he had seen the fox.

"No," he said, but pointed with his finger to the corner inside his hut.

However, the hunters did not understand the hint and believed his word. So they continued along their way at full speed. When the fox made sure that they were out of sight, he departed without saying anything to the woodcutter, whereupon the man scolded him and said, "You ungrateful fellow, is this the way you take leave of your host? You owe your life to me, and yet you leave me without a word of thanks."

"A fine host you are!" said the fox, turning around. "If your deeds had been as good as your words, I would not be leaving your hut without bidding you farewell."

*There is just as much malice in a wink as in a word.*

# LXI

## The Monkey and the Camel

At a great meeting of the beasts, the monkey stood up to dance, and his performance delighted all those present so much that they honored him with great applause. Such praise infuriated the camel, who stood up and tried to show up the monkey with his own dancing. He made such a fool of himself, however, that the beasts became outraged and drove him out of the meeting with clubs.

*Stretch your arm no farther than your sleeve will reach.*

# LXII

## The Dove and the Crow

A dove, locked up in a cage, was congratulating herself on how many children she had hatched, when a crow came by and said, "Stop boasting, my friend! The more young ones you have, the more slaves there will be for you to groan over."

*We must have freedom to enjoy our blessings.*

# LXIII

## The Ass and the Lap Dog

There was once a man who had an ass and a beautiful Maltese lap dog. The ass was kept in a stable and had plenty of corn and hay to eat. Indeed, he was just as well off as any ass could be. The little dog stayed in the house and was a great favorite with the master. He was always playing and frisking about in an amusing way and was permitted to lie in his master's lap. Meanwhile, the ass had plenty to do: he hauled wood all day long and had to take his turn at the mill during the night. He often complained about his misfortunes, and it galled him to see the lap dog living in such ease and luxury, while he had to work so hard. Gradually he convinced himself that if he acted the same way as the lap dog to his master, he would be treated the same way. So, one day he broke from his halter and galloped into the house, where he began to kick and prance about in the strangest fashion. Then, switching his tail and mimicking the antics of the pet lap dog, he knocked over the table where his master was dining. Moreover, he smashed all the dishes to tiny pieces and did not stop until he jumped upon his master, attempting to lick and paw him with his roughshod feet.

Seeing their master in grave danger, the servants thought it was now high time to intervene, and after releasing him from the ass's caresses, they beat the foolish beast with sticks and clubs until he could not get up again. As he breathed his last gasp, he exclaimed, "Why couldn't I have remained satisfied the way I was? Why did I try to imitate a creature who was nothing but an idle puppy after all!"

# LXIV

# The Hares and the Frogs

Since the hares were continually threatened by enemies all around them, they once held a meeting to discuss their sad predicament. Eventually they decided that death would be much more preferable to their desperate condition, and off they went to a nearby lake, determined to drown themselves as the most miserable of creatures.

It so happened that a group of frogs were seated upon the bank, enjoying the moonlight, and when they heard the hares approaching them, they became frightened and leaped into the water in great alarm and confusion. On seeing the rapid disappearance of the frogs, one of the hares cried out to his companions, "Stop, my friends! Our situation is not so desperate as it seems. There are other poor creatures even more fainthearted than ourselves."

*Remember, no matter how miserable you are, there are some people whose shoes you would not want to wear.*

# LXV

# The Fisherman and the Little Fish

One day a fisherman, who earned his living with his nets, caught nothing but one little fish after a long, hard day of work.

"Spare me," pleaded the little creature. "I beg you. I'm so small that I wouldn't be much of a meal for you anyway. I haven't reached my full size yet. If you throw me back into the river, I'll become bigger and will be worth eating. Then you can come here and catch me again."

"Do you take me for a fool?" replied the man. "I've got you now, and if I let you return to the water, your tune will be, 'Catch me, if you can.' "

*Only a fool would pass up a certain gain for an uncertain profit.*

# LXVI

# The Wind and the Sun

The wind and the sun once had an argument as to which was the stronger of the two, and they agreed to settle the issue by holding a contest: whoever could make a traveler take off his coat first would be recognized as the most powerful. The wind began and blew with all his might until he stirred up a blast, cold and fierce as an Alaskan storm. The stronger he blew, however, the tighter the traveler wrapped his coat around him and clasped it with his hands. Then the sun broke out, and with his welcome beams he dispersed the clouds and the cold. The traveler felt the sudden warmth, and as the sun shone brighter and brighter, he sat down, overcome by the heat, and threw his coat on the ground.

Thus the sun was declared the winner, and ever since then, persuasion has been held in higher esteem than force. Indeed, sunshine of a kind and gentle manner will sooner open a poor man's heart than all the threats and force of blustering authority.

# LXVII

# The Farmer and the Stork

A farmer set up a net in his field to catch some cranes that had been constantly feeding upon his newly-sown corn. When he went to examine the net and to see what the cranes had taken, there was a stork among them.

"Spare me!" cried the stork. "I'm not a crane. Nor have I eaten any of your corn. As you can see, I'm a poor innocent stork, the most pious and dutiful of birds. I honor and respect my mother and father. I—"

But the farmer cut him short. "All this may be true enough, but I only know that I've caught you with those birds who were destroying my crops, and since you were sharing their company, you must share their fate."

*Birds of a feather flock together.*

# LXVIII

## The Lioness

Once when all the beasts were arguing among themselves as to which of the animals could produce the largest number of whelps at birth, they went to the lioness and asked her to settle the dispute.

"And how many do you have at birth?" they asked.

"One," she said defiantly, "but that one is a lion."

*No matter how much you have, never argue with quality.*

# LXIX

## The Brash Candlelight

A candlelight that had grown fat and saucy with too much grease boasted one evening before a large gathering that it shone brighter than the sun, the moon, and all the stars put together. Right at that moment, a puff of wind came and blew it out. Someone lit it again and said, "Shine on, friend candlelight, but hold your tongue. The lights of heaven are never blown out."

# LXX

## The Old Woman and the Physician

An old woman, who had become blind, called in a physician and promised him before witnesses that she would reward him most generously if he could restore her eyesight. However, he was to receive nothing if he did not cure her malady. Upon agreeing to these conditions, the physician treated the old lady's eyes from time to time without attempting to make much progress. In the meantime he succeeded in carrying off all her goods little by little. After a few weeks had gone by, he finally set about his task in earnest and cured her, whereupon he requested his reward. But, when the old woman recovered her sight, she saw that her house had been ransacked and continually put off the physician with excuses whenever he demanded payment. Consequently, he summoned her before the judges and charged her with neglect of payment. In her defense, she said, "What this man says is true enough. I promised to reward him if he restored my sight and to give him nothing if he did not heal my eyes. He now maintains that I am cured, but I say just the opposite. When I was first struck by my disease, I could still see all sorts of furniture and goods in my house. But now, even though he asserts that he has restored my eyesight, I cannot see even a tiny trace of my furniture or my possessions."

*He who plays a trick must be prepared to pay the consequences.*

# LXXI

# The Charcoal-Burner and the Cloth-Fuller

A charcoal-burner, who had more room in his house than he needed for himself, proposed to a cloth-fuller to come and share his quarters with him.

"Thank you," said the fuller, "but I must decline your offer, for I fear that as fast as I fill and whiten my goods, you will blacken them again."

*Like will draw like.*

LXXII

# The Wolf and the Sheep

After being attacked by some dogs, a wolf was maimed and could not move. Therefore, when a sheep passed by, he asked her to fetch him some water from a nearby stream. "If you bring me something to drink," he said, "I'll soon be able to find meat for myself."

"Yes," said the sheep. "I have no doubt that you will, for if I come close enough with the water, you'd certainly make me provide you with the meat as well."

*Hypocrisy is close to mendacity.*

# LXXIII

# The Farmer and His Sons

A farmer, who was on the verge of death, wanted to make sure that his sons would overcome their personal quarrels and maintain the farm in a successful way. So, he called them together and said, "My sons, I'm about to depart from this life, and you will find all that I have to leave you in the vineyard."

Some time later, after the old man had died, the sons set to work with their spades and plows, thinking that their father had buried a treasure in the ground. They turned the soil over and over again, but found no treasure. However, the vines, strengthened and improved by this thorough tillage, yielded a finer vintage than they had ever produced before and more than repaid the young farmers for all their trouble. In the end, industry is truly a treasure in itself.

# LXXIV

## The Wolves and the Sheep

Once the wolves sent an embassy to the sheep to make a peace treaty between them for the future.

"Why should we continue such deadly strife?" the wolves asked. "The dogs are the cause of it all. They're constantly barking at us and provoking us. Send them away, and there will no longer be any obstacle to our eternal friendship and peace."

The silly sheep listened, and the dogs were dismissed. As a result, the flock was deprived of their best protectors, and the sheep became an easy prey for their treacherous enemies.

*Change not friends for foes.*

# LXXV

# The Mole and Her Mother

"Mother, I can see," said a young mole to her mother.

In response, the mother put a lump of frankincense before her and asked her what it was.

"A stone," the young one said.

"Oh, my child," said the mother, "not only can't you see, but you can't even smell!"

*Brag about one defect and you'll reveal another.*

# LXXVI

## The Swallow and the Crow

The swallow and the crow had an argument as to which was the finer bird. The crow ended the dispute by saying, "Your feathers may be beautiful and fine during the summer, but mine will protect me and last for many winters."

*Fine-weather friends are not worth much.*

# LXXVII

## The Man Bitten by a Dog

A man who had been bitten by a dog went searching for someone who could cure him. At one point he met a stranger who said, "Sir, if you want to be cured, take a piece of bread and dip it into the blood of the wound. Then give it to the dog who bit you."

The man smiled and replied, "If I were to follow your advice, I would be bitten by all the dogs in the city."

*Whoever proclaims that he is ready to buy up his enemies will never want a supply of them.*

# LXXVIII

# The Man and the Lion

Once while a man and a lion were traveling together, they began arguing about who was the braver and the stronger of the two. Just as their tempers started to flare they happened to pass a statue carved in stone depicting a lion being strangled by a man.

"Look at that!" exclaimed the man. "What more undeniable proof of our superiority can you have than this?"

"That's your version of the story," responded the lion. "If we were the sculptors, there would be twenty men under the paw of a single lion."

*History is written by the victors.*

# LXXVIX

# The Monkey and the Dolphin

It was an old custom among sailors to carry Maltese lap dogs or monkeys to amuse themselves on voyages. So, once while a man had a monkey with him as a companion during a voyage, the ship became caught in a violent storm off the coast of Sunium, the famous peninsula of Attica. After it was capsized, all on board were thrown into the water and had to swim for land as best they could. A dolphin saw the monkey struggling, and thinking that he was a man, whom dolphins are said to befriend, he went to help him and carried him on his back straight for shore. When they were just opposite Piraeus, the harbor of Athens, the dolphin asked the monkey if he were an Athenian.

"Yes," answered the monkey. "Certainly. I'm from one of the first families in the place."

"Then, of course, you know Piraeus," said the dolphin.

"Oh, yes," replied the monkey, who thought it was the name of some distinguished citizen. "He is one of my most intimate friends."

Infuriated by such a gross lie, the dolphin dived to the bottom of the water and left the lying monkey to his fate.

*One lie will lead to another and ultimately seal one's doom.*

# LXXX

## The Dog and His Master

A man was about to set out on a journey when he saw his dog standing at the door. "What are you gaping at?" asked the man. "Get ready to come with me."

Wagging his tail, the dog replied, "I'm all set, master. It's you who has to pack up."

# LXXXI

## The Viper and the File

A viper entered a smith's shop and began looking around for something to eat. At last, he saw a file, and after approaching it, he began nibbling. But the file warned him to stop.

"You're unlikely to get very much from me," he said, "especially since it's my business to bite others."

# LXXXII

# The Bundle of Sticks

A farmer, whose sons were always quarreling with one another, had tried a long time in vain to reconcile them with words. Finally, he decided that he might have more success by setting some sort of an example. So, he called his sons to him and told them to place a bundle of sticks in front of him. Then, after tying them tightly into a bundle, he told them, one after the other, to pick up the bundle of sticks and break it. They all tried, but nothing came of their efforts. Then, the father untied the bundle and gave them the sticks to break one by one, which they did with great ease.

"So it is with you, my sons," said the farmer. "As long as you remain united, you're a match for all your enemies. But if you are divided among yourselves, you'll be broken as easily as these sticks."

*In unity there is strength.*

# LXXXIII

## Jupiter, Neptune, Minerva, and Momus

Jupiter, Neptune, and Minerva (so the story goes) once had a contest to determine which one could make the most perfect thing in the world. Jupiter made a man; Minerva made a house; Neptune made a bull. And Momus—for he had not been banished from Olympus yet—was chosen to judge which of the creations had the greatest merit. He began by finding fault with the bull because its horns were not below his eyes and thus would not be able to see when he butted with them. Next he found fault with the man because there was no window in his breast that would allow his inward thoughts and feelings to be seen. And finally, he found fault with the house because it did not have wheels to enable its inhabitants to move away from bad neighbors. After Momus pronounced all his judgments, Jupiter drove the critic out of heaven and told him that a fault-finder could never be pleased and that he should stop criticizing the works of others until he had created something worthwhile himself.

# LXXXIV

## The Lion in Love

A long time ago a lion fell in love with a woodcutter's daughter and demanded to marry her. The woodcutter was not very pleased by this offer and declined the honor of such a dangerous alliance. When the lion showed his royal displeasure and threatened the poor man, however, the woodcutter realized that such a formidable creature was not to be denied, and he eventually hit upon a clever expedient.

"I feel greatly flattered by your proposal," the woodcutter said. "But, noble sir, what great teeth you have! What great claws you have! Where is a damsel who would not be frightened by such weapons as these? You must have your teeth pulled out and your claws pared before you can be a suitable bridegroom for my daughter."

The lion submitted to these conditions right away (for what won't a man do for love?) and then called upon the father to accept him as a son-in-law. But the woodcutter, no longer afraid of the tamed and disarmed bully, grabbed a stout club and drove the foolish suitor from his door.

# LXXXV

## The Nurse and the Wolf

While roving about in search of food, a wolf passed a door where a child was crying and his nurse was chiding him. As the wolf stood listening, he heard her say, "If you don't stop crying this instant, I'll put you outside, and the wolf will get you."

Thinking the old woman would be as good as her word, the wolf waited quietly outside the house expecting a splendid supper. But when it grew dark, and the child became quiet, he heard the nurse, who was now fondling the child, say, "That's a good boy. Now if that naughty wolf comes, we'll beat him to death!"

Disappointed and mortified, the wolf thought it was now high time to be going home. Indeed, hungry as only a wolf can be, he went along muttering to himself, "This comes from listening to people who say one thing and mean another!"

# LXXXVI

# The Birdcatcher and the Lark

A birdcatcher was setting traps upon a meadow when a lark, who was watching from a distance, asked him what he was doing.

"I'm building a colony," he said, "and I'm laying the foundations for my first city."

After he finished his work, the man retreated to a nearby spot and hid himself. Meanwhile, the lark, who had believed everything he had said, flew down to the place, and after swallowing the bait, found himself caught in the noose. Before he knew what was happening, the birdcatcher came and took him prisoner.

"What a nice fellow you are!" the lark exclaimed. "If this is the kind of colony you build, you won't find many emigrants to settle down in your city."

# LXXXVII

## Jupiter and the Bee

A long time ago when the world was young, a bee had stocked her combs with a bountiful harvest and flew up to heaven to make an offering of honey. Jupiter was so delighted with the gift that he promised to give her whatever she desired. In turn, she responded immediately and said, "Oh glorious Jove, my maker and master, poor bee that I am, give your servant a sting so that when anyone approaches my hive to take the honey, I may kill him on the spot."

Due to his love of man, Jupiter became angry at her request and answered, "Your prayer shall be granted but not the way you wish. Indeed, you shall have your sting, but whenever anyone comes to take your honey and you attack him, the wound shall be fatal not to him but to you, for your life shall go with your sting."

*Whoever wishes harm upon his neighbor will bring a curse upon himself.*

# LXXXVIII

## The Travelers and the Plane Tree

On a hot summer's day, some travelers, worn out by the heat of the sun, noticed a plane tree and rushed toward it. Once they arrived, they threw themselves down on the ground and rested in the shade of its wide spreading branches. As they were lying there, one of the travelers said to the other, "What a useless tree the plane is. It bears no fruit, and there's no other way man can put it to use."

But the plane tree answered them, "Ungrateful creatures! At the very moment you're benefiting from my existence, you deride me as if I were good for nothing!"

*Ingratitude is as blind as it is base.*

# LXXXIX

# The Fox Without a Tail

A fox was once caught in a trap, and the only way he could save himself was by leaving his tail behind him. Knowing that without a tail he would be the laughing stock of all the other foxes, he almost wished that he had died rather than having saved himself. Determined to make the best of a bad situation, he called a meeting of the foxes and proposed that everyone should follow his example.

"You have no idea of the ease and comfort with which I now move about," he asserted. "I would never have believed it if I hadn't tried it myself. But when you really think about it, a tail is such an ugly, inconvenient, unnecessary appendage, and the only wonder is that we, as foxes, could have put up with it so long. Therefore, I propose, my worthy brethren, that you all profit from my wonderful experience and that, from this day on, all foxes should cut off their tails."

When he sat down, a sly old fellow stood up, and waving his long brush with a graceful air, he said, "If I had lost my tail as you did, my friend, your proposal would be very convincing. But until I have such an accident, my vote will always be in favor of keeping our tails."

*Be wary of advice prompted by selfishness.*

## XC

# The Horse and the Stag

A horse once had a whole meadow to himself, but a stag came and damaged the pasture. Anxious to gain revenge, the horse asked a man if he would help him punish the stag.

"Yes," said the man, "but you must let me put a bit in your mouth and get on your back. Then I'll find the weapons to punish the stag."

The horse agreed, and the man mounted him. From that time on, however, instead of gaining revenge, the horse has been the slave of mankind.

*Revenge may be not be worth the price when you pay for it with your liberty.*

# XCI

# The Mischievous Dog

There was once a dog so wild and mischievous that his master was obliged to fasten a heavy collar with a bell around his neck to prevent him from biting and worrying his neighbors. The dog was so proud of his badge that he paraded about in the marketplace, shaking his collar to attract attention. But a sly old friend admonished him, "The less noise you make, the better. Your collar is not a mark of distinction but a sign of disgrace!"

*Men often mistake notoriety for fame.*

# XCII

# The Geese and the Cranes

Some geese and cranes were feeding together in the same field one day, when a bird-catcher suddenly came upon them. Since the cranes were slim and light, they could fly off right away and escape the bird-catcher's nets. The geese, however, weighed down by their fat, could not take off so easily and were all captured.

*Those who are caught are not always the most guilty.*

# XCIII

## The Quack Frog

Emerging from the mud of a swamp, a frog proclaimed to the entire world that he had surfaced to cure all diseases.

"Come and see the most miraculous doctor in the world!" he cried. "No one is my equal, not even Aesculapius himself, Jove's physician!"

"How dare you pretend to be able to heal others," asked the fox, "when you're not even able to cure your own limping gait and blotched and wrinkled skin?"

*A man's professions can only be tested by his practice. Physician, heal yourself!*

# XCIV

## Mercury and the Woodcutter

While chopping down a tree on the bank of a river, a woodcutter let his ax slip by chance into the water, and it immediately sank to the bottom. This accident upset him so much that he sat down by the side of the stream and lamented his carelessness with bitter tears. Fortunately, Mercury, whose river it was, took pity on him and suddenly appeared. After he heard what had happened, he dived to the bottom of the river and brought back a golden ax. Then he asked the woodcutter whether the ax was his. When the man said no, Mercury dived a second time and brought back a silver one. Again the man said that it was not his. Finally, after diving a third time, Mercury produced the ax that the man had lost.

"That's mine!" said the woodsman, delighted to have recovered his ax. And, so pleased was Mercury with the woodcutter's honesty that he promptly gave him the other two as presents.

Later on the woodcutter went to his companions and told them what had happened. One of his friends decided to see whether he would have the same kind of luck. So, he went to the same place as if he intended to cut wood, and he let his ax slip into the water on purpose. Then he sat down on the bank and pretended to weep. Mercury appeared as he had once before, and upon hearing that the man was crying because he had lost his ax, he dived into the river.

When he returned with a golden ax, he asked the man whether it was the ax he had lost.

"Yes, that's definitely the one," said the man eagerly, and he was about to grab the treasure when Mercury not only refused to give this ax to him but would not even return his own. Thus the man was soundly punished for his lying and impudence.

*Honesty is the best policy.*

# XCV

# The Oxen and the Butchers

Once upon a time the oxen held a meeting and decided to do away with the butchers, whose whole art, they said, had been conceived for their destruction. So they sharpened their horns for the battle when a very old ox, who had worked at the plow for a long time, addressed them in the following manner: "Take care, my friends, and make sure you know what you're doing. At least these men kill us with decency and skill, but if we fall into the hands of botchers instead of butchers, we will suffer a double death. Indeed, you can rest assured that men can exist without butchers, but they will never go without beef."

*Do not be in a hurry to exchange one evil for another.*

# XCVI

## The Goatherd and the Goats

It was a stormy day, and the snow was falling fast when a goatherd drove his goats, all covered with white flakes, into a deserted cave for shelter. There he discovered that a herd of wild goats, more numerous and larger than his own, had already taken refuge. The goatherd was so struck by the size and looks of these goats, much more beautiful than his own, that he decided to keep them as well and left his own goats to look after themselves. In fact, he took the branches that he had brought for his own goats and gave them to the wild ones to browse on. When the weather cleared up, however, he found that his own goats had perished from hunger, while the wild goats had run off into the hills and woods. So the goatherd returned to his village, where his neighbors mocked him for having failed to capture the wild goats and for having lost his own in the bargain.

*Whoever neglects old friends for the sake of new deserves what he gets if he loses both.*

# XCVII

# The Widow and the Sheep

Once there was a widow who owned just one sheep. Wishing to make the most of his wool, she sheared him so closely that she cut his skin as well as his fleece. Suffering from such painful treatment, the sheep cried out, "Why are you torturing me like this? What will my blood add to the weight of the wool? If you want my flesh, send for the butcher, who will put me out of my misery at once. But if you want my fleece, send for the shearer, who will clip my wool without drawing my blood!"

*Cutting small costs can cause great wounds.*

# XCVIII

# The Marriage of the Sun

Once upon a time during a very warm summer, word was spread among the animals that the sun was going to be married. All the birds and beasts were delighted at the thought, and above all, the frogs were determined to celebrate. But an old toad put a stop to their festivities by remarking that it was an occasion for sorrow rather than joy.

"If the sun alone can manage to parch our marshes so that we can hardly bear it," he said, "what will become of us if he should happen to have a dozen little suns in addition to himself?"

# XCIX

# The Thief and His Mother

A schoolboy stole a hornbook from one of his schoolmates and brought it home to his mother. Instead of punishing him, she encouraged him and was proud of his deed. In the course of time, the boy, now a grown man, began to steal things of greater value until he was finally caught in the act. Soon thereafter he was tried and sentenced to death. As he was being led toward the place of execution, he noticed his mother in the crowd standing along the way. She was wailing and beating her breast, and he begged the officers for permission to whisper a few words in her ear. When she quickly drew near and placed her ear to her son's lips, he seized the lobe of it tightly between his teeth and bit it off. Immediately she shrieked, and the crowd joined her in scolding the unnatural son, as if his former evil ways had not been enough. Now he had even gone a step further by committing this impious deed against his mother. However, he responded, "It's she who's the cause of my ruin! If she had given me a sound flogging when I stole my schoolmate's hornbook and brought it to her, I would never have grown so wicked and come to this untimely end."

*Nip evil in the bud.*

C

# The Gnat and the Bull

After a gnat had been buzzing about the head of a bull for several minutes, he finally settled down upon a horn and begged the bull's pardon for disturbing him. "If my weight causes you any inconvenience at all," he said, "just tell me, and I'll be off in a moment."

"Oh, don't trouble your mind about that," said the bull. "It's all the same to me whether you go or stay. To tell you the truth, I didn't even know you were there."

*The smaller the mind the greater the conceit.*

# CI

# The Lion, the Bear, and the Fox

A lion and a bear pounced upon a fawn at the same time and had a long, grueling fight over it. The struggle was so hard and even that both of them eventually lay half-blinded and half-dead on the ground without enough strength to touch the prize that was stretched out between them. A fox, who had gone round them at a distance several times, saw how helpless they were, and he stepped in between the combatants and scampered off with the booty.

"What miserable creatures we are!" the lion and the bear cried. "We've knocked ourselves out and destroyed one another merely to give a rogue a dinner!"

*Sometimes one man's toil is another man's profit.*

## CII

# The Oak and the Reed

An oak that had been uprooted by a storm was carried down a river to the banks where many reeds were growing. The oak was astonished to see that things so slight and frail had withstood the storm when so great and strong a tree as he himself had been uprooted.

"It's really not amazing," said a reed. "You were destroyed by fighting against the storm, while we survived by yielding and bending to the slightest breath that was blown."

# CIII

## The Dog in the Manger

A dog made his bed in a manger and kept the horses from eating their food by snarling and growling at them.

"See what a miserable cur that dog is!" said one of the horses. "Even though he himself can't eat the hay, he won't allow anyone else to eat it who can."

*We should not deprive others of their blessings simply because we cannot enjoy them ourselves.*

# CIV

# The Goose with the Golden Eggs

There was once a man who was lucky enough to own a goose that laid him a golden egg every day. However, since the process was so slow and since he wanted the entire treasure at once, he became dissatisfied and eventually killed the goose. After cutting her open, he found her to be just what any other goose would be.

*The more you want, the more you stand to lose.*

## CV

# The Lion and the Dolphin

While roaming along the seashore, a lion saw a dolphin basking on the surface of the water, and he suggested to him that they form an alliance.

"Since I am king of the beasts," the lion said, "and you are the sovereign ruler of all the inhabitants of the ocean, we ought to be great friends and allies, if possible."

The dolphin consented to this proposal, and not long after this, the lion was having a fight with a wild bull and called upon the dolphin for his promised support. Although the dolphin was ready to help the lion, he discovered that he could not come out of the sea to help his ally, and the lion called him a traitor.

"Don't blame me," responded the dolphin. "Blame my nature. No matter how powerful I am at sea, my nature makes me helpless on land."

*In choosing allies, make sure that they are not only willing to help but have the power to do so.*

# CVI

# The Comedian and the Farmer

A wealthy patrician once treated the people of Rome to great theatrical acts and publicly offered a prize to anyone who could perform something unique. Stimulated by this offer, numerous actors arrived from all over the country to compete for the prize, and among them was a well-known, witty comedian, who spread the news that he would do something extraordinary. When the people heard his news, the whole city came together, and the theater could barely hold the number of spectators who came to see the spectacle. When the comedian appeared alone on stage without any props or assistants, curiosity and suspense mounted, keeping the spectators in profound silence. All of a sudden the comedian thrust his head into his bosom and mimicked the squealing of a young pig in such a natural way that the audience believed he had one under his cloak and ordered him to be searched. Yet, once this was done, nothing could be found, and they celebrated this event with the most extravagant applause imaginable.

A farmer was in the audience, and when he witnessed this unique act, he remarked, "Oh, I can do better than that!" And all at once he announced that he would perform the next day.

As a result, an even larger crowd gathered the following day. However, most of the people were biased in favor of the comedian, and they came to laugh at the farmer rather than give him a fair chance. When the two men came out on stage, the comedian grunted away first, and his performance was received with great clapping and applause. Then the farmer pretended that he had concealed a little pig under his clothes (which he had really done) and pinched its ear until he made it squeal.

The people cried out that the comedian had imitated the pig much more naturally and began hooting and demanding that the farmer leave the stage. But to show them how wrong they were, the farmer produced the real pig from his bosom.

"And now, gentlemen," he said, "you can decide for yourselves what sad judges you make!"

*It is easier to convince a man against his senses than against his will.*

# CVII

## The Dog Invited to Supper

A rich gentleman invited a nobleman to dine with him, and extraordinary preparations were made for the repast. At the same time the gentleman's dog met the nobleman's dog, and he, too, said, "Come, my good fellow, and sup with us tonight."

The nobleman's dog was delighted with the invitation and arrived early to watch the preparations for the feast.

"What a splendid meal this will be!" he said to himself. "What good luck! I'll revel in the delicious food, and I'll take good care to store away a few things tonight, for I may have nothing to eat tomorrow."

As he said this to himself, he wagged his tail and gave a sly look to his friend who had invited him. But his wagging tail caught the cook's eye, and he immediately grabbed the strange dog by the legs and threw him out of the window. When the dog landed on the ground, he began yelping and running down the street. Thereupon, the neighbor's dogs ran up to him and asked him how he had liked his supper.

"To tell you the truth," he said with a sorry smile, "I hardly know, for we drank so much that I can't even tell you how I got out of the house."

*Those who enter through the back door can expect to be shown out through the window.*

# CVIII

## The Ass Loaded with Salt

There was once a huckster who kept an ass, and when he heard that some cheap salt was being sold at the seaside, he drove his ass there to buy some. After having loaded the ass with as much salt as it could carry, the huckster drove him home alongside a slippery ledge of rock, until the ass accidentally fell into the river below. When the salt dissolved, the ass was relieved of his burden so that he reached the bank with ease. Then he continued his journey, light in body and spirit. Some time later, the huckster set off for the seashore for some more salt and loaded the ass, if possible, with even more salt than before. On their way home, they crossed the river into which the ass had previously fallen, and this time he slipped into the water on purpose. Once again the salt dissolved, and the ass was relieved of his load. Disturbed by the loss of the salt, the huckster tried to think of a way to cure his ass from performing this trick. So, on his next journey to the coast, he placed a load of sponges on the beast. When they arrived at the same river as before, the ass was up to his old tricks and rolled himself into the water. But the sponges became soaking wet, and the ass discovered to his dismay that his burden had doubled its weight instead of getting lighter.

*The same ploy will not suit all circumstances.*

# CIX

## The Thief and the Dog

A thief who had come to rob a house during the night sought to stop the barking of a dog by throwing pieces of meat to him.

"Get out of here!" said the dog. "I had my suspicions about you before, but this excess of kindness and generosity only confirms my opinion that you are a rogue."

*A bribe in hand betrays mischief at heart.*

# CX

# The Trumpeter Taken Prisoner

A trumpeter, who had bravely led the charging soldiers of his regiment, was taken prisoner in battle and begged hard for mercy from his captors.

"Spare me, good sirs, I beseech you!" he cried. "There's no reason to put me to death. I haven't killed anyone, and I was not carrying any weapons. The only thing I have with me is this trumpet."

"But that's the very reason," said his captors, "why you shall die. Even though you don't fight yourself, your trumpet stirs the soldiers and instills them with a spirit to fight and shed blood."

*He who stirs others to go to war and cause bloodshed is worse than those who take part in it.*

# CXI

## The Hunter and the Fisherman

A hunter was returning from the mountains loaded with game when he met a fisherman coming home with his basket full of fish. The hunter admired the fish and desired to have them for supper, while the fisherman longed to have a meal of game. So they quickly agreed to exchange catches, and from then on they continued to do so every day until a neighbor said to them, "If you keep exchanging your catch so frequently, you'll soon lose the pleasure of your exchange, and you'll each want to keep only what you've caught."

*Pleasure is increased through abstinence.*

# CXII

## The Fir Tree and the Bramble

One day a fir tree was boasting to a bramble, "Your life is really without significance and no use to anyone, whereas mine is filled with many high and noble purposes. How could barns and houses be built without me? I furnish taper spars for ships and beams for roofs of palaces."

"Good sir," replied the bramble, "when the woodcutters come here with their axes and saws, what would you give to be a bramble and not a fir?"

*Better a humble life and security than the dangers that confront the high and mighty.*

# CXIII

## The Eagle and the Arrow

A bowman took aim at an eagle and struck him in the heart. As the eagle turned his head in the agony of death, he saw that the arrow was winged with his own feathers.

"How sharper and more painful," said he, "are the wounds made by weapons we ourselves have supplied!"

# CXIV

# The Two Pots

Two pots, one made of clay, the other of brass, were swept down a river in a flood. The brass pot told his companion to stay by his side, and he would protect him.

"Thank you for your offer," said the clay pot, "but that's just what frightens me. If you'll just keep your distance from me, I'll be able to float down the river in safety. But if we come in contact with one another, I'm bound to be the one who'll suffer."

*Avoid neighbors who are too powerful. If there is a collision, the weaker one will be destroyed.*

# CXV

## The Fisherman and Troubled Water

A fisherman went to a river to fish, and when he had laid his nets, he tied a stone to a long cord and beat the water on both sides of the net to drive the fish into the meshes. One of his neighbors who lived nearby saw him doing this and became upset. Therefore, he went up to the fisherman and reproached him for disturbing the water and making it so muddy that it was unfit to drink.

"I'm sorry about this," said the fisherman, "but it is only by troubling the waters that I can earn my living."

# CXVI

# The Lark and Her Young Ones

There was once a nest of young larks in a field of corn that had just become ripe, and the mother was on the lookout every day for the reapers. Whenever she went in search of food, she told her young ones to report all the news they heard to her. One day, while she was absent, the master came to inspect the condition of the crops.

"It's high time to call together my neighbors and reap my corn," he said.

When the mother lark came home, the young ones told her what they had heard and begged her to remove them from the field right away.

"There's plenty of time," she said. "If he's counting on his neighbors, he'll have to wait a while yet for his harvest."

Next day, however, the owner came again, and finding the sun even hotter, the corn riper, and nothing done, he said, "There's not a moment to lose. Since I can't depend on my neighbors, I must call together my relatives." And, turning to his son, he said, "Go call your uncles and cousins, and see whether they can begin tomorrow."

In greater fear than ever before, the young ones repeated the farmer's words to their mother.

"If that's all there is," she said, "don't be frightened, for the relatives have their own harvest work to finish. But be sure you pay attention to what you hear the next time, and let me know what the farmer says."

The following day the mother went out in search of food, and the owner came once again. Finding that the corn was falling to the ground because it was too ripe, and seeing that nobody was at work, he called to his son.

"We can no longer wait for our neighbors and friends. Go and hire some reapers tonight, and we'll get to work ourselves tomorrow."

When the young ones told their mother what they had heard, she said, "Well then, it's time to be off, for when a man makes up his mind to do his work himself instead of leaving it to others to do, you can be sure that he means to do what he says."

*Self-help is the best help.*

# CXVII

## The Arab and the Camel

After having loaded his camel, an Arab asked the beast whether he preferred to go up hill or down hill.

"Tell me, master," responded the camel, "has someone blocked the straight way across the plain?"

# CXVIII

# The Travelers and the Hatchet

Two men were traveling along the same road when one of them picked up a hatchet and cried, "Look what I've found!"

"Don't say *I*," responded the other, "but look what *we* have found."

Some time later the man who had lost the hatchet appeared and claimed that the man who found it had stolen it.

"Alas," the accused said to his companion, "we are done for."

"Don't say *we*," the other replied, "but *I* am done for. Remember, whoever doesn't let his friend share the prize cannot expect him to share the danger."

# CXIX

## The Doctor and His Patient

A doctor had been treating a sick man for some time when the man died under his care. At the funeral the doctor walked about talking to the relatives and said, "If only our poor friend had refrained from drinking wine and had taken care of his body, he would not be lying here."

"My good sir," one of the mourners responded, "your words are really useless right now. You should have offered these prescriptions when your patient was still alive to take them."

*The best advice may come too late.*

# CXX

# The Maid and the Pail of Milk

A country maid was carrying a pail of milk on her head to the farmhouse when she began daydreaming and musing. "The money that I earn from this milk will enable me to increase my stock of eggs to three hundred. If I take into account that some of these eggs may be rotten and some may be destroyed by vermin, I should be able to get at least two hundred and fifty chickens from them. The chickens should be ready just about the time when the price for poultry is high so that, by the new year, I should have enough money to buy a new gown. Green—let me think—yes, green suits me best, and green it shall be. Then I'll go to the fair in this dress, and all the young fellows will try to win me for a partner. But no—I'll toss my head and refuse every one of them."

Excited and carried away by this thought, the milkmaid could not prevent herself from acting out what she had just imagined in her head, and down came the can of milk and with it all her dreams of happiness vanished in a second!

*It is never wise to count your chickens before they hatch.*

# CXXI

# The Ass, the Fox, and the Lion

After deciding to become partners, an ass and a fox went out into the country to hunt. On the way they met a lion, and realizing the danger ahead, the fox went straight to the lion and whispered, "If you promise not to harm me, I'll betray the ass, and you'll easily have him in your power."

The lion agreed, and the fox managed to lead the ass into a trap. No sooner did the lion capture the ass than he quickly attacked the fox and kept the ass in reserve for his next meal.

*Traitors must expect treachery.*

# CXXII

## The Ass and His Driver

An ass that was being driven along the road by his master suddenly left the beaten track and bolted as fast as he could to the edge of a cliff. When he was just at the point of falling over, his master ran up, grabbed him by the tail, and tried to pull him back. But the ass resisted and pulled the opposite way until the man let go and said, "Well, Jack, if you want to be your own master, I can't help it. A willful beast must go his own way."

# CXXIII

## The Birds, the Beasts, and the Bat

Once upon a time there was a fierce war waged between the birds and the beasts. For a while the outcome of the battle was uncertain, and the bat, taking advantage of his ambiguous nature, kept out of the fray and remained neutral. Finally, when it appeared that the beasts would prevail, the bat joined their side and was active in the battle. The birds rallied successfully, however, and the bat was found among the ranks of the victors at the end of the day. After a peace agreement was speedily concluded, the bat's conduct was condemned by both parties, and since he was recognized by neither side and thus excluded from the terms of the truce, he was compelled to skulk off as best he could. Ever since then he has lived in dingy holes and corners, never daring to show his face except in the dusk of twilight.

*Those who practice deceit must expect to be shunned.*

## CXXIV

# The Hedge and the Vineyard

A foolish young heir, who had just taken possession of his wise father's estate, had all the hedges surrounding his vineyard torn out because they did not bear any grapes. By tearing down these fences, however, he lay his grounds open to man and beast alike, and all his vines were soon destroyed. So the simple fellow learned too late that he cannot expect to gather grapes from brambles and that it is just as important to protect a vineyard as to possess it.

# CXXV

## The Frogs Who Desired a King

A long time ago, when the frogs led a free and easy life in the lakes and ponds, they became disgruntled because everyone lived according to his own whim, and chaos reigned. Consequently, they gathered together and petitioned Jupiter to let them have a king who would bring order into their lives and make them more responsible. Knowing how foolish the frogs were, Jupiter smiled at their request and threw a log down into the lake.

"There is your king!" he declared.

This log made such a splash that it terrified the poor frogs, who dived under water and into the mud. No one dared to come within ten leaps of the spot where it lay in stillness. Eventually, one frog, who was bolder than the rest, ventured to pop his head above the water and watch their new king at a respectful distance. When some others soon perceived that the log was lying stock-still, they began to swim up to it and around it. At last they grew so bold that they leaped upon it and treated it with the greatest contempt. Dissatisfied with such a tame ruler they immediately petitioned Jupiter a second time to grant them a more active king. This time he sent them a stork, and no sooner did the bird arrive than he began seizing and devouring them one by one as fast as he could. Devastated by their new king, the frogs now sent Mercury with a private message to Jupiter, beseeching him to take pity on them once more. But Jupiter replied that they were being justly punished for their folly and that maybe next time they would learn to let well enough alone.

*When you desire to change your condition, make sure that you can really improve it.*

# CXXVI

## The Lion and the Goat

One summer's day, when everyone was suffering from extreme heat, a lion and a goat came to a small fountain at the same time to quench their thirst. They began right away to quarrel as to which one was entitled to drink the water first, and it seemed that each one would resist the other even to the point of death. However, as they rested for a moment during their argument to recover their breath, they noticed a flock of vultures hovering over them and waiting to pounce on the loser. Consequently, they immediately settled the quarrel and agreed that it was far better for them to become friends than to furnish food for the crows and vultures.

# CXXVII

# The Mice in Council

Once upon a time the mice were so distressed by the way a particular cat was persecuting them that they called a meeting to decide upon the best way to get rid of this perpetual annoyance. Many plans were discussed and rejected. At last a young mouse got up and proposed that a bell should be hung around the cat's neck so that they might always know in advance when she would be coming and thus be able to escape her. This proposal was greeted with great applause and approved immediately by everyone at the meeting. Thereafter, an old mouse, who had sat in silence during the entire proceedings, got up and said that he considered the entire plan ingenious and that it would undoubtedly be quite successful. But he still had one short question to put to the other mice: which one of them was to put the bell around the cat's neck?

*It is one thing to conceive of a good plan and another to execute it.*

# CXXVIII

## The Fox and the Mask

A fox had stolen into the house of an actor, and as he was rummaging among the various possessions, he came upon a remarkable mask that was a fine imitation of a human head.

"What a fine looking head!" he cried. "Pity that it lacks brains!"

*Handsome looks are of little worth without sense.*

# CXXIX

## The Thirsty Pigeon

A pigeon was desperate with thirst, and when she saw a glass of water painted on a sign, she thought it was real. So she swept down upon it with all her might and crashed into the board, breaking her wing. As a result, she fell helpless to the ground where she was quickly captured by a bystander.

*Zeal should not outrun discretion, even when we are desperate.*

# CXXX

## The Farmer and the Cranes

Some cranes settled down in a farmer's field that had recently been sown with wheat and made it their feeding grounds. For some time the farmer frightened them away by threatening them with an empty sling. But when the cranes discovered that he was only slinging air, they were no longer afraid of him and would not fly away. Consequently, the farmer slung stones and killed a good number of the birds. In response the rest of the cranes took off and cried out to each other, "It's time for us to be off. This man isn't just threatening us any longer. He's really serious about getting rid of us."

*If words do not suffice, blows must follow.*

# CXXXI

## The Falconer and the Partridge

A falconer caught a partridge in his net, and the bird cried out in sorrow, "Let me go, good falconer, and I promise you that I will serve you as a decoy and attract other partridges into your net."

"No," the man said. "I might have done something else with you, but now I'm definitely not going to spare you. Whoever is ready to betray his friends just to save himself deserves a punishment worse than death."

# CXXXII

## The Cat and the Mice

A cat, who had grown feeble with age, was no longer able to hunt mice as she used to do. So, she tried to think of new ways to entice them within reach of her paws. Finally, it occurred to her that she might be able to pass herself off for a bag or, at least, for a dead cat, if she hung herself by her hind legs from a rafter in the hope that the mice would no longer be afraid to come near her. An old mouse, who was wise enough to keep his distance, whispered to a friend, "Many a bag have I seen in my day, but never one with a cat's head."

"Hang there, my good lady, as long as you please," said the other. "For my part, I wouldn't come within reach of you, even if you were stuffed with straw."

*Even when danger may not appear threatening, it is wise to avoid it.*

# CXXXIII

# The Father and His Two Daughters

A man who had two daughters married one to a gardener and the other to a potter. After a while he paid a visit to the daughter who had married the gardener, and asked her how she was and how everything was going.

"Excellent," she replied. "We have everything we want. Our only need right now is a heavy rainfall to provide water for our plants."

Then the father went off to visit the daughter who had married the potter and asked her how everything was.

"There's not a thing we need," she responded, "and I only hope that this fine weather and hot sun may continue so that our tiles will bake well."

"Alas," said the father, "if you wish for fine weather, and your sister, for rain, how can I reconcile the two?"

# CXXXIV

## The Heifer and the Ox

A heifer that ran wild in the fields and had never felt the yoke derided an ox at plow for submitting himself to such labor and drudgery. The ox said nothing but went on with his work. Not long after this incident, there was a great festival. The ox was granted a holiday, but the heifer was led off to be sacrificed at the altar.

"If this is the reward for your idleness," the ox said, "then I think my work is more rewarding than your play. Indeed, I'd rather have my neck feel the yoke than the ax."

# CXXXV

# The Fox and the Hedgehog

While crossing a river, a fox was driven by the current into a narrow gorge and lay there exhausted for a long time, unable to get out. To add to his misfortune, a swarm of horseflies settled all over his body and began bothering and stinging him. A hedgehog, who came wandering in that direction, saw him and offered out of pity to drive away the flies that were tormenting him so much. However, the fox begged him to do nothing of the sort.

"Why not?" asked the hedgehog.

"Because these flies who have attached themselves to me right now are already full and draw very little blood," he explained. "If you were to remove them, a swarm of fresh, hungry rascals would take their place, and I would not have a drop of blood left in my body."

*By ridding ourselves of rulers or dependents who have already taken the most out of us, we often lay ourselves open to others who will make us bleed even more blood than before.*

# CXXXVI

## The Lion and the Ass

A lion and an ass agreed to go out hunting together, and after some time had passed, they came to a cave where wild goats were dwelling. The lion took his position at the mouth of the cave while the ass entered and began to kick, bray, and make a great fuss to frighten the goats out. When the lion had caught a good deal, the ass came out and wanted to know whether the lion thought he had fought nobly and routed the goats in a proper fashion.

"Yes, indeed," said the lion, "and I can assure you that you would have frightened me too, if I had not known you to be an ass."

# CXXXVII

## The Bald Knight

Once there was a knight who was growing old, and his hair was falling out. When he became bald, he decided to hide this imperfection by wearing a wig. One day, as he was out hunting with some friends, a sudden gust of wind blew off the wig and exposed his bald head. His companions could not stop themselves from laughing at the accident, and he himself laughed as loud as anyone.

"How should I have expected to keep strange hair on my head," he remarked, "when my very own won't stay there anymore?"

# CXXXVIII

# The Ass and His Masters

An ass, who belonged to a gardener and had little to eat but much to do, prayed to Jupiter to release him from the gardener's employ and provide him with another master. However, Jupiter was angry that the ass was discontent and placed him in the service of a potter. Now the ass had a greater burden to bear than before and appealed to Jupiter once more to lighten his work. So, Jupiter intervened and had him sold to a tanner. Once the ass realized what kind of work his new master did, the ass uttered a sorrowful moan: "Alas, wretch that I am! I would have been better off if I had remained content with my former masters. Not only will my new owner work me harder while living, but he won't even spare my hide when I am dead!"

*Whoever is dissatisfied in one place will seldom be happy in another.*

# CXXXVIX

## The Farmer and the Sea

Seeing a ship full of sailors being tossed about on the waves of the sea, a farmer cried out, "Oh sea, how deceitful and merciless you are! You can look so inviting and then you destroy all who venture out upon you!"

The sea heard him and, disguising his voice as that of a woman, replied, "Why are you reproaching me, kind sir? It's not me who has caused this storm, rather the winds. When they fall upon me, they give me no rest. But if you should sail over me when they are away, you'll see that I'm more mild and more tractable than your own Mother Earth."

# CXL

# The Hart and the Vine

A hart, who was mercilessly pursued by hunters, hid himself among the branches of a vine. When the hunters passed by without discovering him and he thought that the coast was clear, he began browsing upon the leaves that had concealed him. But one of the hunters, attracted by the rustling of the leaves, turned around, and guessing where their prey was, shot into the bush and killed him. As the hart was dying, he uttered these last words: "This is what I justly deserve for being so ungrateful and injuring the vine that protected me when I was in danger."

# CXLI

# The Pig and the Sheep

A young pig, hoping to avoid the slaughterhouse, set up quarters in a fold of sheep. One day the shepherd grabbed hold of him, and he squeaked and struggled with all his might to get away. The sheep reproached him for making such a commotion and said, "The master often grabs hold of us, and you don't see us crying."

"That's true," replied the pig, "but our situation is not the same. He catches you for your wool, while he's after me for frying."

# CXLII

## The Bull and the Goat

Once when a bull was being pursued by a lion, he fled into a cave where a wild goat was living. The goat was an ornery creature and began attacking the bull by butting him with his horns.

"If I put up with this now," the bull said, "don't suppose it's because I'm afraid of you. Once the lion is out of sight, I'll soon show you the difference between a bull and a goat."

*Never approach mean people when in distress.*

# CXLIII

# The Old Man and Death

An old man who had traveled a long way with a huge bundle of sticks became so weary that he threw his bundle down on the ground and called upon death to deliver him from his most miserable existence. Death came straight to his side and asked him what he wanted.

"Please, good sir," he said, "do me a favor and help me lift my burden again."

*It is one thing to call for death and another to see him coming.*

# CXLIV

## The Dog and the Hare

After discovering a hare in some bushes, a dog pursued her for a long time, biting her with his teeth as if he would take her life and also licking her as if he were playing with another dog. Not knowing what to make of this, the hare stopped running and said, "I wish you'd show your true colors. If you're a friend, why do you bite me so hard? If an enemy, why caress me?"

*A dubious friend is worse than a true enemy.*

# CXLV

## The Boy and the Hazel Nuts

Once a boy put his hand into a bottle containing a lot of hazel nuts and figs. He grabbed as many as his fist could possibly hold, but when he endeavored to pull his hand out, he was hampered because the neck was too narrow. Unwilling to lose any of his treasure, but unable to draw out his hand, he burst into tears and lamented his hard fortune. Then a wise friend who stood nearby came to his aid by giving him the following advice: "Grab only half right now, and the other half later, and you're bound to succeed."

*Do not attempt too much at once.*

# CXLVI

# The Wolf and the Shepherd

A wolf followed a flock of sheep for a long time and made no attempt to attack them. However, the shepherd had his suspicions, and for a while he was always on his guard against him, knowing that the wolf was an avowed enemy of the sheep. But when the wolf stayed close to the flock day after day without trying to seize any one of them, he began to regard him more as a friend than a foe. Then, one day, when he had to go to town, he decided to entrust the sheep to his care. However, no sooner did the wolf accept this responsibility then he fell upon the sheep and devoured them. Upon his return, the shepherd found his flock destroyed and exclaimed, "What a fool I am! But this is what I deserve for trusting a wolf with my sheep."

*With friends like wolves you don't need enemies.*

# CXLVII

# The Jackass and the Statue

An ass who was carrying a statue in a religious procession was driven through a town, and all the people bowed in deep reverence as the statue passed them. As a result the ass, who thought that they were actually worshipping him, became very much taken with himself and refused to budge another step. But the driver soon laid the stick across his back and said, "You foolish dolt! They're not paying you their respect but the statue that you're carrying."

*Only fools try to take the credit due to others.*

# CXLVIII

# The Blacksmith and His Dog

There was once a blacksmith who had a little dog. While he hammered away at his metal, the dog slept. But whenever he sat down to have dinner, the dog woke up.

"You sluggard!" cried the brazier, throwing him a bone. "You sleep through the noise of the anvil, but wake up at the first clatter of my teeth."

*People are always awake when food is on the platter, but they often turn a deaf ear when called to work.*

# CXLIX

## The Herdsman and the Lost Calf

A herdsman, who had lost a calf, went roaming through the forest intent on finding it. After a long and fruitless search, he made a vow to all the nymphs of the forest and the mountains, as well as to Mercury and to Pan, that he would sacrifice a lamb to them if they would help him discover who stole his calf. Not long afterwards, as he reached the summit of a hill, he saw a lion feeding on the calf. And now the unhappy man vowed to sacrifice a full-grown bull along with the lamb if the gods would only let him escape from the thief's clutches.

*If all our rash vows were to be granted, many of us would be ruined by our requests.*

# CL

# The Lion and the Other Beasts Who Went Out Hunting

The lion and other beasts formed a party to go out hunting. After they had killed a fat stag, the lion nominated himself to divide the stag into three parts. Taking the best piece for himself, he said, "This is mine in view of my official role as king, and the second I'll take as my own personal share just for participating in the hunt. As far as the third part is concerned, let him take it who dares."

# CLI

# The Bees, the Drones, and the Wasp

Some bees had built their comb in the hollow trunk of an oak tree. However, the drones claimed that they had done all the work and the comb belonged to them, not the bees. They brought their case to court before judge wasp, who knew something about both parties and thus addressed them as follows: "The plaintiffs and the defendants are so much alike in shape and color that the rights to the ownership of the comb are indeed questionable, and the case has been properly brought before me. Therefore, I order that each party take a hive to itself and build a new comb so that the lawful proprietors of the property in dispute may be determined from the shape of the cells and the taste of the honey."

The bees readily assented to the wasp's plan, but the drones declined. As a result, the wasp declared, "It is now clear who made the comb and who cannot make it. The court grants the honey to the bees."

*Professions are best tested by deeds.*

# CLII

# The Kid and the Piping Wolf

A kid who had strayed from the herd was pursued by a wolf. When he saw that there was no hope of escape, he turned around and said to the wolf, "I must admit, indeed, that I am your victim, and since my life will now be very short, let it be a merry one. So, please pipe a tune for me, and I will dance."

While the wolf was piping and the kid was dancing, the dogs heard the music and ran to see what was going on. When they saw the wolf, they immediately began chasing him, and the wolf took off as fast as his legs would carry him.

*Whoever goes out of his way to play the fool should not be surprised if he loses face.*

# CLIII

# The Stallion and the Ass

Adorned with his fine trappings, a stallion, who was on his way to war, came thundering along the road and aroused the envy of a poor ass, who was trudging along the same route with a heavy load on his back.

"Get out of my way," cried the proud horse, "or I'll trample you under my feet!"

The ass said nothing but quietly moved to one side to let the horse pass. Not long after this incident, he met the same horse on the same road but in different circumstances. The stallion had been wounded in battle, and his master killed. He himself was now lame, half blind, and obliged to carry a heavy load by a new master, who drove him along with brutal blows of a whip.

*The path of contempt is not without its pitfalls.*

# CLIV

## The Mice and the Weasels

The mice and the weasels had been at war with each other for a long time. Since the mice had continually got the worse of the battle, they gathered together at a solemn meeting, where they agreed that their defeats were due to nothing but a lack of discipline. Therefore, they decided to elect regular commanders for the future and chose those whose valor and prowess were suitable for the important positions. The new commanders were proud of their positions and desired to be as conspicuous as possible. So, they put horns on their foreheads as a sort of crest and mark of distinction. Not long after this, the battle with the weasels resumed. Just as before, the mice were soon put to flight. The common soldiers escaped into their holes, but the commanders were hampered by their horns, and every one of them was caught and devoured.

*There is no distinction that does not bring some kind of danger with it.*

# CLV

## The Stubborn Goat and the Goatherd

After a stubborn goat had strayed from the herd and stood on the edge of a high rock nibbling grass, the goatherd did his best to bring him back to his companions. He tried calling and whistling without success, and at last, having lost his patience, he picked up a stone and struck one of the goat's horns, causing it to break. Alarmed at what he had done, the goatherd begged the goat not to tell his master what had happened, but the goat replied, "How foolish can you be! Even if I keep quiet about this incident, my horn will tell the story."

*Facts speak plainer than words.*

# CLVI

## The Boys and the Frogs

Some boys were playing at the edge of a pond when they noticed a number of frogs in the water and began pelting them with stones. They had already killed many of the poor creatures when one of the frogs, more courageous than the rest, lifted his head out of the water and cried out to them, "Stop your cruel game, my boys! What you think is play is death to us."

*What we do in sport often causes great trouble for others.*

# CLVII

# The Mouse and the Weasel

A lean and hungry mouse had made his way into a basket of corn with some difficulty. He found the fare so good, and he stuffed himself with such a voracious appetite that, when he wanted to get out of the basket, he found the hole too small to allow his bloated body to pass through, push as hard as he might. As he sat at the hole groaning about his fate, a weasel, who had amused himself by watching the vain struggles of the fat little thing, called and offered the following advice: "Listen to me, my plump friend. There is only one way to get out, and that's to wait until you're just as lean and hungry as you were when you entered."

# CLVIII

## The Farmer and the Lion

One day a lion entered a farmyard, and the farmer shut the gate, intent on catching him. When the lion discovered that he could not get out, he began at once to attack the sheep and then the oxen. So the farmer, now scared about his own life, opened the gate, and the lion made off as fast as he could. His wife, who had observed the entire scene, watched her husband moaning about the loss of his cattle, and she cried out, "You deserve what you got! How could you have been crazy enough to try to catch a lion? Under ordinary circumstances, if you saw him at a distance, you'd wish that he were even further away."

*Better scare a thief than snare him.*

# CLIX

# The Horse and the Loaded Ass

There was once a man who owned a horse and an ass. Whenever he took trips, he tended to spare the horse and put all the burden on the ass's back. Since the ass had been ailing for some time, he asked the horse one day to relieve him of part of his load while on a trip.

"If you take a fair portion of the load," he said, "I'll soon get well again. But if you refuse to help me, this weight will kill me."

The horse, however, told the ass to get on with it and to stop troubling him with his complaints. The ass jogged on in silence, but he was soon overcome by the weight of his burden and dropped dead in his tracks, just as he had predicted. Consequently, the master came up, untied the load from the dead ass, put it on the horse's back, and made him carry the ass's carcass in addition.

"That's what I get for my bad disposition!" the horse groaned. "By refusing to pull my own weight, I now have to carry all of it along with some dead weight in the bargain."

*Laziness often results in an additional burden for its own back.*

# CLX

## The Wolf and the Lion

One day, after a wolf had killed a sheep and was carrying it home to his den, he met a lion, who immediately grabbed the sheep from the wolf and dragged it away. Standing at a safe distance from the lion, the wolf howled at the lion and told him that he should be ashamed of himself for robbing him. The lion laughed and said, "I suppose, then, that it was your good friend the shepherd who gave you the sheep in the first place."

*One thief is no better than the next.*

# CLXI

## The Farmer and the Dogs

During a severe winter, a farmer was snowed in his farmhouse. When he found that he could not procure any food outside, he began consuming his own sheep. As the hard weather continued, he began to eat his goats. And finally—for there was no break in the weather—he turned to the plow oxen. Thereupon, the dogs said to one another, "We'd better be off! If the master has no pity on the oxen, who carry the burden of the work around here, it's highly unlikely that he'll spare us."

*When our neighbor's house is on fire, it is time to save our own skin.*

# CLXII

# The Eagle and the Crow

A crow watched an eagle swoop down with majestic air from a nearby cliff, descend upon a flock of sheep, and then carry off a lamb in his talons. The whole thing looked so graceful and easy that the crow was eager to imitate it. So, he swept down upon a large, fat ram with all the force he could muster and expected to carry him off as a prize. His claws became entangled in the wool, however, and as he tried to escape, he fluttered and made such a commotion that he drew the shepherd's attention, enabling the man to seize him and clip his wings. That evening the shepherd brought the bird home to his family, and his children asked, "What kind of bird is this, Father?"

"Well," he said, "if you were to ask him, he would tell you that he's an eagle. But if you will take my word for it, I know him to be nothing but a poor crow."

*Sometimes ambition can lead us beyond the limits of our power.*

# CLXIII

# The Lion and His Three Councillors

The lion called the sheep to him to ask her if his breath smelled. She said yes, and he bit off her head for being a fool. He called the wolf and asked him as well. The wolf said no, and the lion tore him to pieces for being a flatterer. Finally he called the fox and asked him the same question. However, the fox apologized profusely and told the lion that he had somehow caught a cold and could not smell.

*Wise men say nothing in dangerous times.*

# CLXIV

## The Great and Little Fish

As a fisherman was drawing in his net that he had cast into the sea, he noticed that it was full of all sorts of fish. However, little fish escaped through the meshes of the net and swam back into the deep water, while the big fish remained trapped and were hauled into the boat.

*It is not always smart or safe to be a big fish in a small pond.*

# CLXV

## The Ass, the Cock, and the Lion

An ass and a cock lived together in a farmyard. One day a hungry lion passed by and saw the ass in such good condition that he decided to make a meal out of him. Now, they say that nothing irritates a lion so much as the crowing of a cock, and at that moment the cock happened to crow. So, the lion ran away as fast as he could. Greatly amused to think that a lion would be frightened by a mere bird, the ass plucked up courage, galloped after him, and felt proud that he was driving the king of beasts out of the farmyard. He had not gone very far, however, when the lion turned around sharply and made mincemeat out of him within seconds.

*Presumption begins in ignorance and ends in ruin.*

# CLXVI

## The Wolf and the Goat

A wolf saw a goat grazing on the top of a high cliff where he could not get at her. Pretending to be concerned for her safety, the wolf advised her to move down. "You might lose your footing at that dizzy height," he said. "Besides, the grass is much sweeter and more plentiful here below."

"I'm sorry I can't oblige you," answered the goat, "but the grass isn't always greener on the other side of the hill, especially when you intend to make a meal out of me there."

# CLXVII

# The Fox and the Stork

One day a fox invited a stork to dinner, and since he wanted to amuse himself at the expense of his guest, he provided a meal that consisted only of some thin soup in a large flat dish. The fox was able to lap this soup up very easily, while the stork, unable to take a mouthful with her long narrow bill, was as hungry at the end of dinner as when she began. Meanwhile, the fox pretended to regret seeing her eat so sparingly and feared, so he said, that the dish might not be tasty enough for her. The stork said little but requested the honor of allowing her to invite him to her place in the near future. He was delighted with the invitation, and a week later, he showed up punctually at the stork's home, where the dinner was served right away. To the fox's dismay, however, he found that the meal was contained in a narrow-necked vessel down which the stork easily thrust her long neck and bill, while he was obliged to content himself with licking the neck of the jar. Unable to satisfy his hunger, he left as graciously as possible, observing that he could hardly find fault with his host, who had only paid him back in his own coin.

*Those who mistreat others with their cunning must expect to suffer from it in return.*

# CLXVIII

## The Leopard and the Fox

One day a leopard and a fox had a contest to decide who was the handsomer of the two. The leopard boasted about the beauty of its innumerable spots. But the fox replied, "You may have beautiful spots, but it's better to have a versatile mind than a variegated body."

# CLXIX

## The Vine and the Goat

There was once a vine teeming with ripe fruit and tender shoots and looking forward to the day when it would provide a bountiful vintage. Suddenly a wanton goat appeared and gnawed its bark and nibbled its young leaves.

"You have no right to harm me like this," said the vine. "But I won't have to wait long for my just revenge. Even if you crop my leaves and cut me down to my root, I shall provide the wine to pour over you when you're brought as a sacrifice to the altar."

*Though it may be late, retribution arrives in the end.*

# CLXX

## The Sick Lion

When the lion reached a ripe old age, he became weak and could no longer hunt for his prey. All he could do was to lie in his den, where he breathed with great difficulty. Soon he made it known that he was indeed very ill, and the news was spread among the beasts, who lamented his sick condition. One after the other they came to see him, and one after the other they fell into the lion's trap in his den, where he made an easy prey of them and grew fat on this diet. The fox suspected that there was some foul play and decided to visit the lion and inquire about his health. Standing at some distance, he asked his majesty how he was.

"Ah, my dearest friend," said the lion, "is it you? Why are you standing so far away from me? Come, sweet friend, and whisper a word of consolation in the poor lion's ear, who has but a short time to live."

"Bless you," said the fox, "but you'll excuse me if I cannot stay. To tell you the truth, I feel quite uneasy when I look at the marks left by the footsteps that I see here. They all point toward your den, and none reveal that they have ever left."

*Never venture into an affair unless you know that there is a way out.*

# CLXXI

## The Rivers and the Sea

Once upon a time the rivers joined together and went in one body to the sea.

"Why is it," they accused her, "that after we rivers pour our fresh and sweet waters into you, you immediately make them salty and unpalatable?"

Fully aware of their bad tempers, the sea merely answered, "If you do not wish to become salt, please keep away from me altogether."

*Those who benefit most from a good arrangement are often the first to complain.*

# CLXXII

## The Blackamoor

Once a man bought a blackamoor and assumed that the color of the slave's skin was due to the neglect of his former master. No sooner did he bring him home than he procured all kinds of scouring utensils, scrubbing brushes, soaps, and sandpaper and set to work with his servants to wash him white again. For hours they drenched and rubbed him, but it was in vain. His skin remained as black as ever, while the poor wretch almost died from the cold he caught from all their scrubbing and washing.

*It is not humanly possible to change what is humanly natural.*

# CLXXIII

# The Boy and the Nettle

A boy who was playing in the fields was stung by a nettle. He ran home to his mother and told her that he had merely touched the nasty weed and it had stung him.

"It was just your touching it, my boy," said his mother, "that caused it to sting you. The next time you meddle with a nettle, grab it tightly, and it will not harm you."

*Whatever you do, do it boldly.*

# CLXXIV

## The Seaside Travelers

As some travelers were making their way along a seashore, they came to a high cliff, and looking out at the sea, they saw a log floating at some distance. At first they thought it must be a large ship, and so they waited in hope of seeing it enter the harbor. But as the log drifted nearer to the shore, they no longer thought it was a ship but a small boat. Finally, when it reached the beach, they saw it was nothing but a log and realized that all their watching and waiting had been in vain.

*Our mere anticipations of life outrun its realities.*

# CLXXV

## The Boy Who Went Swimming

A boy was swimming in a river and went so far out that he was in danger of drowning. Fortunately, he saw a man walking by and yelled to him with all his might. Instead of rushing to his aid, however, the man began to lecture the boy for being so foolhardy and swimming in deep water. Finally, the boy was forced to cry out, "Please, sir, save your sermon for later, and save me now."

*Advice without practical help leads nowhere.*

# CLXXVI

## The Sick Hawk

A hawk, who had been very ill for a long time, said to his mother, "Don't cry, Mother. Do me a favor and pray to the gods so that I may recover from this dreadful disease and pain."

"Alas, child!" the mother said. "Which one of the gods do you think will pity you? Is there one whom you haven't outraged by robbing the sacrifices placed at their altars?"

*A deathbed repentance will not suffice to make amends to the errors of a lifetime.*

# CLXXVII

## The Monkey and the Fishermen

A monkey was sitting high up in a tree when he saw some fishermen laying their nets in a river. No sooner did the men set their nets and retreat a short distance to eat something than the monkey came down from the tree, thinking that he would try his hand at the same sport. But in attempting to lay the nets, he got so entangled in them that he almost choked to death and was forced to cry out, "This serves me right! What business did I have meddling with such tackle like this when I don't know the first thing about fishing?"

# CLXXVIII

## Venus and the Cat

There was once a cat who fell in love with a young man and prayed to Venus to change her into a girl, hoping to win his affections. The goddess felt compassion for the cat and transformed her into a fair damsel. As a result, the young man fell in love with the beautiful young woman and eventually took her home as his bride. When they were sitting in their room, Venus wanted to know whether she had changed the cat's nature by changing her shape, and so she set a mouse down before her. Forgetting her human condition, the damsel jumped from her seat and pounced on the mouse as if she would have eaten it on the spot. Disturbed by such a horrendous act, the goddess immediately turned her back into a cat again.

*Try as one may, it is impossible to deny one's nature.*

# CLXXIX

## The Three Tradesmen

Once there was a city expecting to be attacked, and accordingly, a meeting was called to discuss the best means to defend it. A bricklayer claimed that brick was the best way to fortify the city. A carpenter suggested that timber was better. Finally a currier stood up and said, "Sirs, when all is said and done, there is nothing in the world like leather."

*Every man for his trade.*

# CLXXX

## The Ass's Shadow

One hot summer's day, a traveler hired an ass to carry him from Athens to Megara. At noon the sun's heat was so scorching that he dismounted and wanted to relax under the ass's shadow. But the driver of the ass claimed that he had equal rights to the spot and wanted to sit there, too.

"What!" cried the traveler. "Didn't I hire the ass for the entire journey?"

"Yes," answered the driver, "you hired the ass but not the ass's shadow."

While they were arguing and fighting for the place, the ass took to his heels and ran away.

*In quarreling about the shadow of things we often lose the substance.*

# CLXXXI

## The Eagle and the Beetle

Pursued by an eagle, a hare took refuge in the nest of a beetle, whom he begged to save him. The beetle felt compassion for the hare and pleaded with the eagle not to kill the poor creature. In the name of mighty Jupiter, the beetle requested that the eagle respect his intercession and the laws of hospitality even though he was nothing but a tiny insect. However, the eagle became furious and gave the beetle a flap with his wing. In cold blood he seized the hare with his enormous talons and devoured him right on the spot.

When the eagle flew away, the beetle followed him to find out where his nest was. Then he crawled in and rolled the eagle's eggs out, one by one, breaking them in the process. Grieved and enraged to think that anyone would do such an audacious thing, the eagle built his next nest in a higher place. But there, too, the beetle managed to get to it and destroyed the eggs as he had done before.

The eagle was now at a loss as to what to do. So he flew up to Jupiter, his lord and king, and placed the third brood of eggs as a sacred deposit in his lap, begging him to guard them for him. However, the beetle made a little ball of dirt and flew up with it to Jupiter and dropped it on his lap. When Jupiter saw the dirt, he stood up right away to shake it off, forgetting the eggs, which were again broken as they rolled off his lap. The beetle now informed Jupiter that he had done this to gain revenge on the eagle, who had not only wronged him but had acted with impiety toward Jove himself. Therefore, when the eagle returned, Jupiter told him that the beetle was the wronged party and that his complaint was not without justification. Nevertheless, Jupiter did not want the race of eagles to be humiliated, so he advised the beetle to arrange a peaceful settlement with him. But the beetle would not agree to this, and Jupiter was compelled to change the eagle's breeding time to another season when there are no beetles to be seen.

*No matter how powerful one's position may be, there is nothing that can protect the oppressor in the end from the vengeance of the oppressed.*

# CLXXXII

## The Lion and the Three Bulls

Three bulls were such great friends that they always grazed together in the same field. A lion had watched them for many days with longing in his eyes in the hope of seizing them for his prize, but he found that there was little chance so long as they all kept together. Therefore, he secretly began to spread evil and slanderous rumors pitting one against the other until he had fomented jealousy and distrust among them. No sooner did the lion see that they avoided one another and grazed separately than he attacked them one by one and made an easy prey of them all.

*United we stand, divided we fall.*

# CLXXXIII

# The Old Woman and Her Maids

A thrifty old widow had two hired maids whom she used to call to work at the first crow of the cock. The maids hated getting up so early in the morning and decided to wring the cock's neck, since he was the one who woke their mistress and was the cause of all their misery. No sooner had they done away with the cock than the old lady became disoriented. Afraid of over-sleeping, she began mistaking the time of day and rousing the unfortunate maids at midnight.

*Too much cunning can undermine its purpose.*

# CLXXXIV

## The Dogs and the Hides

Some dogs, famished with hunger, saw some cowhides that a skinner had left in the bottom of a stream and tried desperately to get them. Since they were unable to reach them, however, they decided to drink up the stream to obtain the hides. Unfortunately they all burst from drinking before they ever came close to the hides.

*Those who attempt the impossible through foolish means are bound to destroy themselves.*

# CLXXXV

## The Dove and the Ant

An ant went to a fountain to quench his thirst, but he tumbled in and began to drown. Fortunately, a dove happened to be sitting on a nearby tree and saw the ant's predicament. So she plucked a leaf off the tree and let it drop into the water. The ant climbed on top of it and was soon washed safely ashore. Shortly afterward a bird catcher came by, spread his net, and was about to ensnare the dove when the ant bit his heel. The man let out a cry and dropped his net. Realizing that she was in danger, the dove flew safely away.

*One good turn deserves another.*

# CLXXXVI

## The Old Lion

A lion, worn out with age, lay stretched out on the ground, utterly helpless and gasping its last breath. A boar, who wanted to satisfy an old grudge, approached him and attacked him with his tusks. Next a bull decided to seek his revenge and bored him with his horns. Realizing that the lion could now be treated with impunity, an ass thought he would show his spite, too, and kicked his heels in the lion's face. Thereupon the dying beast called out to the ass, "The insults of the powerful were bad enough, and somehow I've managed to bear them. But to be spurned by such a base creature as you, who are a disgrace to nature, is to die a double death."

# CLXXXVII

## The Wolf and the Shepherds

A wolf looked into a hut and saw some shepherds enjoying a joint of mutton in great comfort.

"If they had caught me enjoying such a supper," he remarked, "there'd certainly be hell to pay."

*Men often tend to condemn others for the very things that they themselves practice.*

# CLXXXIII

## The Ass in the Lion's Skin

After putting on a lion's skin, an ass roamed about and amused himself by frightening all the foolish animals he encountered. Upon meeting a fox, he tried to scare him as well, but once Reynard heard his voice, he said, "I would've been frightened, too, but your braying gave you away."

*Those who assume a character not suited to them generally betray themselves by overacting.*

# CLXXXVIX

# The Swallow in Chancery

A swallow built her nest under the eaves of a court of justice, and before her young ones could fly, a serpent slid out of his hole and ate them all up. When the poor bird returned to her nest and found it empty, she began to wail in a most pitiful way. However, a neighbor sought to comfort her by remarking that she was not the first bird who had lost her young.

"True," she replied, "but it is not only my little ones whom I mourn, but the fact that I was wronged in the very place to which the injured fly for justice."

CXC

# The Raven and the Swan

A raven was jealous of a swan's white feathers, and he thought that her beauty was due to the water in which she lived. Therefore, he deserted the altars, where he used to find his livelihood, and flew to the ponds and streams. After arriving, he plumed himself and washed his coat, but it was all in vain. His feathers remained as black as ever, and he himself perished because he could not find his customary food.

*Change of scene cannot bring about a change of nature.*

## CXCI

# The Wild Boar and the Fox

A wild boar was whetting his tusks against a tree when a fox came by and asked him why he was doing this. "I see no reason," he remarked. "There are no hunters nor hounds in sight. In fact, at the moment I can't see any danger at all."

"True," responded the boar, "but when that danger does arise, I'll have other things on my mind than sharpening my weapons."

*It is too late to whet the sword when the trumpet sounds to draw it.*

# CXCII

# The Stag at the Pool

One summer's day a stag came to a pool to quench his thirst, and as he stood drinking, he saw his form reflected in the mirror. "How beautiful and strong my horns are!" he remarked. "But how weak and unseemly these feet of mine are!"

While he was examining and criticizing the features that nature had given him, the hunters and hounds drew near. The feet, with which he had found so much fault, soon carried him out of reach of his pursuers, but the horns, which were his pride and joy, became entangled in a thicket and kept him from escaping so that the hunters caught up with him and took his life.

*We tend to underestimate the small things about ourselves that are often our most valuable attributes.*

# CXCIII

## The Wolf in Sheep's Clothing

Thinking that it would be easier to earn a living if he disguised himself, a wolf put on a sheep's skin. Soon afterward he managed to slip into a flock of sheep and graze among them so that even the shepherd was fooled by his disguise. When night came and the fold was closed, the wolf was locked in with the sheep. But the shepherd needed something for his supper, and as he went to fetch one of the sheep, he mistook the wolf for one of them and killed him on the spot.

# CXCIV

## The Boasting Traveler

A man who had traveled widely in foreign countries returned home and was always bragging and boasting about the great feats he had performed in different places. Among other things he said that, when he was in Rhodes, he had made such an extraordinary leap that no man could come close to it, and he had witnesses there to prove it.

"Possibly," said one of his listeners, "but if this is true, there is no need of witnesses. Just suppose this is Rhodes and try the leap again."

*The best way to cure a boaster is by putting his words to the test.*

# CXCV

## The Man and His Two Wives

There was once a time when a man was allowed more wives than one, and a middle-aged bachelor, who could be called neither young nor old, and whose hair was just beginning to turn gray, fell in love with two women at the same time and married them both. One was young and lively and wanted her husband to look youthful; the other was somewhat more advanced in age and was concerned that her husband look about the same age as she did. So, the young wife seized every opportunity to pull out all her dear husband's gray hairs, while the older one zealously plucked out every black hair she could find. For a while the man was highly flattered by their attention and devotion until, one morning, he discovered that, thanks to his two wives, he did not have a hair left on his head.

*Whoever allows his principles to be swayed by the influence and different needs of conflicting parties will end in having no principles at all.*

# CXCVI

## The Shepherd and the Sea

A shepherd moved his flock down near the seashore so that the sheep could graze there, and as he looked at the sea lying in a smooth and breathless calm, he was overcome by a strong desire to sail over it. So he sold all his sheep and bought a cargo of dates. Then he loaded a vessel with the dates and set sail. He had not gone very far when a storm arose. His ship was wrecked, and his dates and cargo were lost. He himself had great difficulty escaping the sea and reaching land. Not long after this incident, when the sea was calm again, one of his friends, who had joined him on a walk along the seashore, began admiring its repose.

"Watch out, my good fellow," the shepherd remarked. "That smooth surface is only on the lookout for your dates."

# CXCVII

## The Miser

To make sure that his property would always remain safe and protected, a miser sold all that he had and converted it into one great lump of gold, which he hid in a hole in the ground. Since he went there continually to visit and inspect it, one of his workers became curious and suspected that his master had hidden a treasure. When the miser's back was turned, the worker went to the spot and stole the gold. Soon thereafter the miser returned, and when he found the hole empty, he wept and tore his hair. But a neighbor, who witnessed his grief, told him, "Don't fret any longer. Just take a stone and put it in the same place. Then imagine that it's your lump of gold. Since you never meant to use it, the stone will be just as good as the gold."

*The value of money depends not on accumulation but in its use.*

# CXCVIII

# Mercury and the Sculptor

Once Mercury wished to learn what men thought about him. So he disguised himself as a traveler and entered a sculptor's workshop, where he began asking the price of the different statues he saw there. Pointing to an image of Jupiter, he asked how much the sculptor wanted for it.

"A drachma," said the sculptor.

Mercury laughed up his sleeve and asked, "How much for this of Juno?"

The man wanted a higher price for that.

Mercury's eye now caught sight of his own statue. "Most likely this fellow will ask ten times the price for this," he thought. "After all, I'm heaven's messenger and the source of all his gain." So he asked the sculptor once more what he wanted for the statue of Mercury.

"Well," said the man, "if you give me what I ask for the other two, I'll throw this into the bargain for nothing."

*Those people who are too anxious to know what the world thinks of them will seldom fetch the price they set upon themselves.*

# CXCIX

# The Miller, His Son, and Their Ass

A miller and his son were driving their ass to a nearby fair to sell him. They had not gone far when they came across a group of girls returning from town. They were in a merry mood, talking and laughing, and when they saw the miller and his son, one of them cried out, "Look there! Did you ever see such fools like those two, trudging on foot when they could be riding!"

Upon hearing this, the old man told his son to get on the ass while he walked along cheerfully by his side. Soon they came to a group of men who were having a serious argument.

"There!" said one of them. "That proves what I was saying. There's no more respect shown to the old nowadays. Do you see that young loafer riding while his old father has to walk? Get down, you miserable creature, and let the old man rest his weary limbs!"

Upon hearing this, the father made his son dismount and then got on the ass himself. They had not proceeded very far when they met a company of women and children.

"Why, you lazy old fellow!" cried several tongues at once. "How can you ride that beast, while that poor little lad there can hardly keep pace with you."

The good-natured miller stood corrected and immediately had his son mount behind him. They were now about to reach the town, when a townsman said, "Tell me, friend, is that ass your own?"

"Yes," answered the old man. "Oh! I wouldn't have thought so by the way you've loaded him down. Why, you two fellows are better suited to carry the poor beast than he you!"

"Anything to please you," said the miller. "It wouldn't hurt to try."

So, dismounting with his son, they tied the ass's legs together, and with the help of a pole, they attempted to carry him on their shoulders over a bridge that led to the town. They made such an amusing sight that the people ran out in crowds to laugh at them. However, the ass neither liked the noise nor his situation and began kicking at the ropes that bound him to the pole. As a result, he tumbled off the pole and fell into the river. Thereupon, the old man, angry and ashamed, made his way home as best he could, convinced that by endeavoring to please everybody he had pleased nobody and lost his ass in the bargain.

## CC

# The Wolf and the Horse

Once when a wolf was roaming all over a farm, he came to a field of oats. But he was not able to eat the oats and thus went on his way. Soon he encountered a horse and told him to come with him into the field.

"I've found some splendid oats," he said, "and I've not even touched a single one. In fact I've saved them all for you, for the very sound of your teeth is like music to my ears."

However, the horse replied, "A fine fellow you are! If wolves were able to eat oats, I'm sure you would have indulged your belly and forgotten about the music for your ears."

*No need to express gratitude to those who only give away what is of no use to them in the first place.*

# CCI

## The Astronomer

An astronomer used to walk around outside every night to watch the stars. One time, as he was wandering on the outskirts of the city and gazing at the stars, he fell into a well. After hollering and crying for help, someone ran up to the well, and after listening to his story, remarked, "My good man, while you are trying to pry into the mysteries of heaven, you overlook the common objects that are under your feet."

# CCII

# The Hunter and the Woodcutter

A man who went out to hunt lions in a forest met a woodcutter, and he asked him whether he had seen any lion's tracks and whether he knew where the lion's lair was.

"Yes," said the man, "and if you'll come with me, I'll show you the lion himself."

Upon hearing this, the hunter turned ghastly pale, and his teeth began to clatter. "No, thank you," he said. "It was the lion's tracks that I was hunting, not the lion himself."

*It is easy for the coward to be a hero at a distance.*

# CCIII

## The Fox and the Crow

A crow had snatched a large piece of cheese from a windowsill and was now perched securely on a high tree, about to enjoy her prize. A fox spied the dainty morsel in her beak and tried to think of a way to make it his.

"Oh crow," he said, "how beautiful your wings are! How bright your eyes! How graceful your neck! Indeed, your breast is the breast of an eagle! Your claws—I beg your pardon—your claws are a match for all the beasts of the field. Oh, if only your voice were equal to your beauty, you would deserve to be called the queen of birds!"

Pleased by the flattery and chuckling as she imagined how she would surprise the fox with her caw, she opened her mouth—and out dropped the cheese, which the fox promptly snapped up. Then, right before he departed, he cried out to the crow, "You may indeed have a voice, but I wonder where your brains are."

*Whoever listens to the music of flatterers must expect to pay the piper.*

# Afterword

Whoever Aesop may have been, he understood the notion of "survival of the fittest" and made it famous centuries before Darwin transformed it into a scientific theory. In fact, the essence of the Aesopian fable depends on the terse metaphoric manner that he developed to counsel listeners how to remain alive in a world in which the "fittest" rule according to might makes right.

Aesop was by no means the inventor of the fable, although he became identified with it and played a major role in shaping the classical structure that has come down to us today. Fables were derived from beast tales in Mesopotamia more than 4000 years ago and spread throughout the Orient and the Mediterranean. These tales involved animal worship, warnings about the dangers of powerful animals, and allegories about natural phenomena that drew parallels between animals and humans, based on their particular traits. When and why these animal tales became fables is difficult to say since we do not possess enough historical evidence and documents that would enable us to ascertain how and why changes occurred in the animal tales. But it is clear that the fable is not a "typical" animal tale or purely an animal tale, and that the fable may have a great deal to do with the rise of slave societies and slave language.

Clearly, the narrative strategy of a fable is to demonstrate how the weak and weak-minded will be exploited and destroyed if they do not learn how to fend for themselves. Although there may be references to

Greek and Roman gods, the fable is secular. It is not bound ideologically to a religious system, nor are the morals based on absolute notions of good and evil or divine commandments. The messages and warnings stem from the experiences of the oppressed, and these people, the "misfits," employed animals and inanimate objects in oral tales as ciphers in a symbolical code, probably out of necessity, for they were fearful of speaking the direct truth about particular oppressors and yet desirous of spreading truthful antidotes to counter the poison of oppression. Historically, fables were first and foremost oral antidotes to tyranny and slavery and became established as a literary genre when conditions allowed for more freedom of speech in script.

This brings us back to Aesop and the legends about this extraordinary storyteller. According to the sparse evidence about his life, gathered from a fictional account and references to him in various Greek works, Aesop was born either in Sardis, the capital of Lydia, on Samos, a Greek island, or in Cotiaeum, the chief city of a province of Phrygia and lived from about 620 to 560 B.C. Most descriptions of him portray the man as hunchbacked and ugly. Moreover, he supposedly had a speech impediment. As a slave, he was owned by a citizen named Iadmon on the island of Samos and was allegedly given his freedom due to his wisdom and wit in helping his master settle disputes. At one point, after becoming counselor to Croesus of Sardis and taking an active part in public affairs, he moved to Athens, ruled at that time by the tyrant Peisistratus, an enemy of free speech, who severely punished all those who opposed his regime. By this time Aesop had become famous for employing fables metaphorically to expose the unjust ways of tyrants. Evidently he insulted Peisistratus, who stirred up the citizens of Delphi, or he offended the Delphians by depriving them of gold. Whatever the true case may have been, it appears that Aesop was condemned to death for sacrilege by the Oracle of Delphi and was thrown over a high cliff at Hypania.

There are other versions of Aesop's life, none of which can be absolutely substantiated. However, we do know that, whether invented or not, through Greek legend, Aesop came to stand for a sophisticated storyteller, who rose from slavery to speak words of wisdom to the common people, and who left a great literary heritage that has spread far beyond the Greek world.

Aesop never wrote down his fables. They survived by word of mouth, and when free speech was established in the Greek city-states after his death, rhetoricians began using the fable to teach scholars style and rules of grammar and to discuss morals and ethics in debates. Many references to Aesop and his fables can be found in the works of Aristophanes, Plato, Aristotle, and other Greek writers. By 300 B.C. Demetrius Phalereus, a distinguished Athenian statesman and orator, founded the Alexandria Library and collected about 200 fables in Greek prose under the title *Assemblies of Aesopic Tales*. Since these fables were often used by Alexandrian grammarians and scribes in their teachings, they became known throughout the Mediterranean, and at the beginning of the Christian era, Phaedrus, a Greek slave, who was freed by Augustus, imitated them in Latin iambics. In the meantime fables from India, associated with another "legendary" storyteller named Kasyapa, formed the basis of the Libyan fables of "Kybises" and were combined with Aesopian fables by a rhetorician named Nicostratus at the court of Marcus Aurelius. Then, in 230 B.C. Valerius Babrius, tutor to the son of Alexander Severus, took 300 of the Aesopian and Libyan fables and turned them into Greek verse with Latin meters. Rhetoricians and philosophers became accustomed to giving the fables as exercises to their students and disciples. The morals of the fables were to be discussed and interpreted. Rules of style and grammar were to be learned through the fables, and the young scholars were encouraged to create new fables, which can be found in isolated works during the early years of the Roman Empire. The major work of this period was the Roman Avianus' collection of 42 fables in Latin verse, based primarily on Babrius' work.

During the Middle Ages, it was primarily the Aesopian fables of Phaedrus, generally turned into prose, which were used by educators and priests in primers and sermons. In addition, Phaedrus' fables served as the basis for various collections in the ninth century by Romulus and in 1030 by Ademar of Chabannes. The fables of Babrius were also transformed into Greek prose and were translated into Arabic. After the Third Crusade these fables, expanded by 60 new ones from the Arabian writer Bidapi, were translated by an Englishman named Alfred. Some of Alfred's fables, attributed to Aesop, were translated into English verse, and in 1200 Marie de France adapted them in French.

In 1480, after the invention of printing, the first significant book of Aesop's fables and his life appeared in German by Heinrich Steinhöwel. He brought together various fables by Romulus, Avian, Babrius, and Alfred. In addition, he included a legendary biography of Aesop and tales by Petrus Alphonsi and Poggio Bracciolini. Within 20 years his book was translated into French, Italian, Dutch, and Spanish. The most important edition for the English-speaking world was Caxton's collection of 1484, and from this point on it was largely Caxton and some version of Steinhöwel's work that passed for Aesop's fables in English. Of course, numerous writers imitated and wrote their own fables, continuing Aesop's tradition up through the twentieth century. Among the more famous western authors, who created unique works, are Jean de la

Fontaine, Jonathan Swift, John Gay, Benjamin Franklin, Gottfried Ephraim Lessing, Lorenzo Pignotti, Tomas de Yriarte, Ivan Andreyevich Kriloff, Ralph Waldo Emerson, Leo Tolstoy, Ambrose Bierce, Robert Louis Stevenson, Oscar Wilde, James Thurber, Jean Anoulih, Alberto Moravia, and William Steig.

The purpose of most fable writers has been to address a *specific* social problem of their times and to draw a *universal* lesson that may be applicable in other situations and epochs. It is this combination of the *specific* with the *universal* that makes the fable so appealing as a lesson, for listeners and readers gain a sense of community and solidarity and learn that they are not alone in their predicament. The fable tells life as it is, the *Realpolitik* of life, with a wry sense of humor, frankness, and clarity. Unlike other related genres of narrative—the fairy tale, legend, or parable—the fable does not offer a happy end or conciliation. At best, the protagonists of an Aesopian fable are lucky if they *escape* with their lives at the end.

However, the Aesopian fable is not totally cynical or pessimistic. It is rather sober and revelatory. In describing the injustice of a situation or deceit, the fable reveals the strengths and weaknesses of the protagonists, while simultaneously exposing the power relations of the world determined by the category of "might makes right." By showing the limits of the underdogs and disadvantaged creatures in a particular exemplary situation, the fable demarcates the true boundaries of freedom. And it is freedom from oppression that the fable preaches and pursues, even though it does not promise a better world or ideal justice.

Almost all the Aesopian fables involve animals and begin with a simple description of the beast's condition that is often the cause for a predicament or will create a predicament. The resolution of this predicament will depend on how wisely the animal acts. It is only through cunning that a creature can counter force and survive. And survival along with revenge are about the most the protagonists can hope to achieve—together with wisdom, of course. Though Aesop clearly sided with the oppressed creatures (i.e., the slaves and the common people), he often showed how the victims victimized themselves through stupidity. In fact the worst crime one can commit in an Aesopian fable is a foolish act. Aesop never forgives stupidity, conceit, arrogance, or vanity. Nor does he stereotype the animals by identifying them with one constant trait. Certainly, he relies on the major observable trait of an animal, but he also will vary it. For instance, though the lion is by far the most powerful beast in the world, he shows wisdom when he refuses to fight a human. (*The Archer and the Lion*) and stupidity when he disarms himself to win a woman (*The Lion in Love*). Quite often the lion uses his power selfishly (*The Lion and the Ass*, and *The Lion, the Bear, and the Fox*), but he also acts graciously at times to help small people (*The Lion and the Mouse*). The fox may be cunning for the most part (*The Fox and the Crow* and *The Fox and the Goat*), but he also learns humility (*The Fox and the Stork* and *The Fox Without a Tail*). Wolves are generally gluttons (*The Wolf and the Lamb*), but they also know when to curb their appetite (*The Wolf and the Lion*). Horses are both vain and humble (*The Stallion*), and dogs are submissive (*The Domesticated Dog*) and surly (*The Dog in the Manger*). Some little animals show unexpected remarkable traits such as the brave beetle in (*The Eagle and the Beetle*) and the gracious ant (*The Dove and the Ant*), while others demonstrate how ludicrous they can be, such as the jealous ass (*The Ass and the Lap Dog*) and the foolish frogs (*The Frogs Who Desired a King*).

Most of the tales that make use of animals or animals and humans center on the theme of exploitation, whereas the fables which focus solely on humans tend to make an ironic comment on some aspect of human nature. Thus *The Astronomer* mocks the ivy-tower intellectual; *The Bald Knight* pokes fun at a man's vanity; *The Comedian and the Farmer* ridicules the mass spectacle; *The Farmer and His Sons* shows how one can determine what real wealth is; *Mercury and the Woodcutter* presents a lesson in honesty. It seems that Aesop felt more inclined to conceal his critique of oppressors in tales which were "peopled" with animals rather than humans, and as I have suggested, this was probably a device that the common people and other storytellers had developed before him. It is to Aesop's credit, however, that he brought this oral genre to fruition.

And it is to Aesop that we owe some of the most enduring fables of western culture. *The Ants and the Grasshopper, The Country Mouse and the Town Mouse, The Hare and the Tortoise,* and *The Shepherd Boy and the Wolf* have all become classics and adapted in extraordinary ways by writers, musicians, artists, and filmmakers for modern audiences and readers. Finally, without intending this in the least, Aesop played a major role in the development of children's literature. As we know Aesop's fables were part of the curriculum in ancient schools and used to teach rules of grammar and composition. In addition, depending on how the fables were adapted during the Middle Ages (i.e., their suitability to Christian thought in Europe), they were also considered beneficial for the moral education of the young. Although Caxton's version of the Aesopian fables was not intended for children, it was gradually adapted as a type of spelling primer and regarded suitable for children because the narratives were so rational and clearly educational. By the end of the eighteenth century, John Newberry, the first major publisher of children's books in England, edited *Fables in Verse for the Improvement of the*

*Young and the Old* (1757) by Abraham Aesop Esq., and from that point on, thousands of juvenile editions have been published in the English-speaking world.

Important in most of the collections of Aesop's fables have been the illustrations, whether intended for children or adults. Among some of the gifted artists who have contributed unusual illustrations for editions of Aesop's fables and La Fontaine's, which are based on Aesop's work, are Marcus Gheeraerts, H. Gravelot, J. I. Grandville, Gustav Doré, Ernest Griset, Randolph Caldecott, Walter Crane, Charles H. Bennett, Arthur Rackham, David Jones, Stephen Gooden, and Marc Chagall. Depending on the personal interpretation of the artist, the illustrations cover a spectrum of moods including dark despair, bitter cynicism, joyous frivolity, ironic mockery, and serious sobriety.

Despite the fact that illustrators and adapters of Aesop's fables have used great poetic license, they have always been compelled to respect Aesop's penetrating gaze into a dark side of human beings portrayed as animals in a dog-eat-dog world. In this respect, their works have generally posed a question that forms the basis of most of Aesop's fables: can human beings rise above animals? Or what is the difference between humanity and bestiality? Aesop was wise enough not to provide an answer, but it is apparent that as long as humans enslave other humans, there is no clear answer, and fables peopled with beasts will continue to speak to the human situation.

—Jack Zipes
*Minneapolis, 1992*

# Selected Bibliography


Blackham, H. J. *The Fable as Literature.* London: Athlone, 1985.

Blount, Margaret. *Animal Land: The Creatures of Children's Fiction.* London: Hutchinson, 1974.

Darton, F. J. Harvey, as revised by Brian Alderson. *Children's Books in England.* Cambridge: Cambridge University Press, 1982.

Hodnett, Edward. *Aesop in England: The Transmissions of Motifs in Seventeenth-Century Illustrations of Aesop's Fables.* Charlottesville: University of Virginia Press, 1979.

Hobbs, Anne Stevenson, ed. *Fables.* London: Victoria and Albert Museum, 1986.

Holzberg, Niklas and Christine Jackson-Holzberg, tr. *Ancient Fable: An Introduction.* Bloomington: University Press of Indiana, 2002.

Jackson, Mary V. *Engines of Instruction, Mischief, and Magic.* Lincoln: University of Nebraska Press, 1989.

Jacobs, Joseph. "A Short History of the Aesopic Fable" in *The Fables of Aesop.* Ed. Joseph Jacobs. New York: Macmillan, 1950.

Klingender, Francis Donald. *Animals in Art and Thought to the End of the Middle Ages.* London: Routledge and Kegan 1971.

Leibfried, Erwin. *Fabel.* 4th ed. Stuttgart: Metzler, 1982.

Lewis, Jayne Elizabeth. *The English Fable: Aesop and Literary Culture, 1651–1740.* Cambridge: Cambridge University Press, 1996.

Lindner, Hermann, ed. *Fabeln der Neuzeit. England, Frankreich, Deutschland.* Munich: dtv, 1978.

Noel, Thomas. *Theories of the Fable in the Eighteenth Century.* New York: Columbia University Press, 1975.

Patterson, Anne. *Fables of Power: Aesopian Writing and Political History.* Durham: Duke University Press, 1991.

Perry, Ben Edward. *Studies in the Text History of Aesop.* Vol. VII. Haverford, PA: American Philological Society, 1936.

Wheatley, Edward. *Mastering Aesop.* Gainesville: University of Florida Press, 2000.

# Index

Ants and Grasshopper, 27
Arab and Camel, 163
Archer and Lion, 18
Ass and Driver, 169
Ass and Grasshopper, 66
Ass and Lap Dog, 95
Ass and Masters, 191
Ass, Cock, and Lion, 224
Ass, Fox, and Lion, 168
Ass in Lion's Skin, 225
Ass Loaded with Salt, 151
Ass's Shadow, 243
Astronomer, 272

Bald Knight, 189
Bear and Fox, 38
Bees, Drones, and Wasp, 207
Belly and Members, 85
Birdwatcher and Lark, 123
Birds, Beasts, and Bat, 170
Blackamoor, 233
Blacksmith and Dog, 203
Blind Man and Whelp, 87
Boasting Traveler, 261
Boy and Hazel Nuts, 199
Boy and Nettle, 234
Boy and Scorpion, 23
Boy Who Went Swimming, 237
Boys and Frogs, 213
Brash Candlelight, 102
Bull and Goat, 195
Bundle of Sticks, 118

Cat and Mice, 183
Charcoal-Burner and Cloth-Fuller, 104
Cock and Jewel, 41
Comedian and Farmer, 147
Country Mouse and Town Mouse, 53
Crab and Mother, 68
Creaking Wheels, 44
Crow and Pitcher, 77

Doctor and Patient, 165
Dog and Hare, 198
Dog and Master, 116
Dog and Shadow, 55
Dog, Cock, and Fox, 39
Dog in Manger, 144
Dog Invited to Supper, 149
Dogs and Hides, 249
Dolphins and Sprat, 86
Domesticated Dog and Wolf, 50
Dove and Ant, 251
Dove and Crow, 93

Eagle and Arrow, 157
Eagle and Beetle, 245
Eagle and Crow, 221
Eagle and Fox, 22

Falconer and Partridge, 181
Farmer and Cranes, 180
Farmer and Dogs, 219
Farmer and Lion, 215

Farmer and Sea, 192
Farmer and Snake, 46
Farmer and Sons, 107
Farmer and Stork, 99
Father and Two Daughters, 184
Fawn and Mother, 28
Fighting Cocks and Eagle, 57
Fir Tree and Bramble, 155
Fisherman and Little Fish, 97
Fisherman and Music, 49
Fisherman and Troubled Water, 159
Flies and Honey Jar, 32
Fox and Crow, 275
Fox and Goat, 25
Fox and Grapes, 15
Fox and Hedgehog, 187
Fox and Lion, 43
Fox and Mask, 178
Fox and Stork, 227
Fox and Woodcutter, 91
Fox Without Tail, 127
Frog and Ox, 45
Frogs Who Desired King, 173

Geese and Cranes, 130
Gnat and Bull, 140
Goose with Golden Eggs, 145
Goatherd and Goats, 136
Great and Little Fish, 223

Hare and Hound, 74
Hare and Tortoise, 65
Hares and Frogs, 96
Hart and Vine, 193
Hawk and Pigeons, 21
Hedge and Vineyard, 171
Heifer and Ox, 185
Hen and Cat, 62
Hercules and Wagoner, 90
Herdsman and Lost Calf, 204
Horse and Groom, 29
Horse and Loaded Ass, 217
Horse and Stag, 128
Hunter and Fisherman, 154
Hunter and Woodcutter, 273

Jackass and Statue, 202
Jupiter and Bee, 124
Jupiter and Camel, 69
Jupiter, Neptune, Minerva, and Momus, 119

Kid and Wolf, 20
Kid and Piping Wolf, 208

Lamb and Wolf, 67
Lark and Young Ones, 161
Leopard and Fox, 228
Lion and Ass, 188
Lion and Dolphin, 146
Lion and Fox, 47
Lion and Goat, 175
Lion and Mouse, 79
Lion and Other Beasts Who Went Hunting, 205
Lion and Three Bulls, 247
Lion and Three Councillors, 222
Lion, Ass, and Fox Who Went Hunting, 83
Lion, Bear, and Fox, 141
Lion in Love, 121
Lioness, 101

Maid and Pail of Milk, 167
Man and Lion, 113
Man and Satyr, 59
Man and Two Wives, 263
Man Bitten by Dog, 112
Marriage of Sun, 138
Mercury and Sculptor, 268
Mercury and Woodcutter, 133

Mice and Weasels, 211
Mice in Council, 177
Miller, Son, and Ass, 269
Mischievous Dog, 129
Miser, 267
Mole and Mother, 110
Monkey and Camel, 92
Monkey and Dolphin, 115
Monkey and Fisherman, 239
Moon and Mother, 56
Mountain in Labor, 31
Mouse and Frog, 71
Mouse and Weasel, 214
Mule, 61

Nurse and Wolf, 122

Oak and Reed, 143
Old Hound, 26
Old Lion, 252
Old Man and Death, 197
Old Woman and Maids, 248
Old Woman and Physician, 103
Old Woman and Wine Bottle, 63
One-Eyed Doe, 80
Oxen and Butchers, 135

Pear, Apple, and Blackberry, 73
Pig and Sheep, 194

Quack Frog, 131

Raven and Swan, 257
Rivers and Sea, 232

Sea Gull and Hawk, 42
Seaside Travelers, 235
Shepherd and Sea, 265
Shepherd Boy and Wolf, 72
Sick Hawk, 238
Sick Lion, 231
Sick Stag, 89
Stag at Pool, 259
Stag in Ox Stall, 75
Stallion and Ass, 209
Stubborn Goat and Goatherd, 212
Swallow and Crow, 111
Swallow in Chancery, 256

Thief and Dog, 152
Thief and Mother, 139
Thirsty Pigeon, 179
Three Tradesmen, 242
Tortoise and Eagle, 60
Travelers and Bear, 84
Travelers and Hatchet, 164
Travelers and Plane Tree, 125
Trees and Ax, 81
Trumpeter Taken Prisoner, 153
Two Bags, 33
Two Pots, 158

Vain Crow, 35
Venus and Cat, 241
Vine and Goat, 229
Viper and File, 117

Widow and Sheep, 137
Wild Boar and Fox, 258
Wind and Sun, 98
Wolf and Crane, 17
Wolf and Goat, 225
Wolf and Horse, 271
Wolf and Lamb, 37
Wolf and Lion, 218
Wolf and Sheep, 105
Wolf and Shepherd, 201
Wolf and Shepherds, 253
Wolf in Sheep's Clothing, 260
Wolves and Sheep, 109
Woman and Fat Hen, 19